MERCY KILLS

Jeff Oliver

A Madness Heart Press Publication

Madness Heart Press
2006 Idlewilde Run Dr.
Austin, Texas 78744

This is a work of fiction. Names, characters, places, and incidents either are the product of the author's imagination or are used fictitiously. Any resemblance to actual persons, living or dead, events, or locales is entirely coincidental.

Cover by Luke Spooner
isbn: 978-1-955745-67-3

First Edition
www.madnessheart.press

Chapter 1

It's always time for my sister to kill. You see, she's a stand-up comedian. Oh, and she's also a trained killer.

Take Thanksgiving back when we were kids. If Mercy wasn't making our parents cackle using the turkey baster to tell a crude insemination joke, she was dazzling everyone with carving skills that were skillful and precise. Nine years-old, adorable in pink glasses, curly hair in pom-poms, slicing up a bird like a master butcher while riffing that Grandma was fake-napping to avoid dish duty. To say Mercy was the favorite would be like saying mom's delicious turkey gravy only slightly improved dad's Sahara-dry vegan stuffing.

It was pretty unfair for me, the glum teenage brother whose only talent was wearing black and frowning. My brilliant way of getting attention during the holidays was to carve Billie Eilish lyrics into my leg and putting it on Tik Tok. It was a move that got me shipped off to a special boarding school for therapy cases two states away. No more Thanksgiving for me. And boy did I miss my little sister. See, despite my petty jealousies at all the attention she got, I'd have done anything to stay with Mercy and laugh at her crazy jokes all day.

Because Mercy was funny in every situation. Even deadly situations, I would soon learn…

See, ten years later I'm one of the first people to have heard her famous "Prison Confession Tape," or as she called it, "Death Row Unplugged." It was smuggled out of a top-secret detention center that no one can even find on a map. By chance the recording landed in my hands, the lowly transcriber of The Resistance. It's how I know that even locked up—cold, bloody, and bruised—Mercy never stopped telling jokes.

"Ever hear the one about the stand-up comic on death row? They say she killed. Or wait… she's a known bomber. Or… maybe she already died onstage? Ugh, bear with me folks, this is my first-time doing comedy in solitary confinement. Is this thing even on? But you're a nice crowd: cold pavement floor, metal toilet, blinking security camera. Not much for looks, but I've performed in Cleveland. And all you want is a confession, right? Or as it was explained to me, 'Confess or else!' Wonder what 'or else' means? More torture? One-ply toilet paper? Middle seat on a Spirit Airlines flight? Blueberry bagels? Stop me if I'm getting warm... Or just taze me."

On and on. And why not? Mercy was caught trying to expose a government conspiracy to enslave the sick, so she's in deep trouble. Lucky for her she's got me, her underappreciated but somehow still-free older brother to tell her story. And it's an epic. Coming-of-age-meets-thriller. And yes, there's a love story mixed in, but I personally find it kinda gross. So here goes. The year is 2034, a full decade after Mercy was just a cute kid joking around at Thanksgiving. And while the whole country is now a fascist dumpster fire spiraling into an authoritarian port-o-potty, Mercy's onstage with a microphone trying to make people laugh. So I'm going to take a backseat and give my sister the respect she deserves. And since this is Mercy we're talking about, might as well start off with a joke?

Chapter 2

"A man walks into a doctor's office and says he feels awful. The doctor takes a look and says, 'I'm afraid you're dying, and you don't have much time.' The man is shocked: 'Doctor, how long do I have?' The doctor says, 'Ten.' So he says, 'Ten what? Ten months? Ten weeks?' And the doctor says, 'Nine. Eight. Seven. Six…'" That's Mercy on stage doing a joke probably written a hundred years ago. Forehead oily and shining in the crudely harsh spotlight, curly hair in her trademark pom-poms, pit stains on a threadbare t-shirt. Why distract the crowd by showering? Wait, here's her twist: "When I first heard that joke I thought, what would I do with those last six seconds? Because for me it's not even a question. I'd take the first half-second and text back my Ex from high school: 'No, Derek, *your* breath smells like Funions.' Then I'd take another half-second to regret some of the bathing suits I've worn. Then I'd take out my belly button ring. Don't want the coroner to think I'm freaky and do weird sexual stuff to my corps. *Or do I?* Finally, I'd use my entire last three seconds to solve a Rubik's Cube. Exactly point-one-three seconds faster than the world record. And then I'd die. And

I'd die happy because I know that the doctor would have to report my death in a way he hadn't counted on seconds before. My obituary would no longer be 'Mercy Gorrison, mediocre open mic comic, died at 3:18pm on Tuesday…' It would be, 'Guinness Book Of World Record-holding Champion of Rubik's Cube fastest-solve, Mercy Gorrison, died at 3:18pm on Tuesday, the exact moment she beat the world record. The heights of her celebrity were short-lived. The rest of her nineteen years were unremarkable. As one friend described: 'She did some *okay* open mics.'"

Mercy awaits the inevitable standing ovation, but she settles for an appreciative belch from one of the drunks slumped over a half-empty beer.

"You've been a great crowd," Mercy lies and walks off stage.

Azeem, who kind of looks like Benedict Cumberbatch if he was from Pakistan, takes over. "Big hand for the Dark Lord of comedy herself, Mercy Gorrison. If I was her doctor, I would've sped up that diagnosis. 'Two… one… dead!' I'm evil! Okay, next comedian up is rising comic sensation, Colby Foster. Give him a big Hilarity Hut welcome."

Mercy grabs her canvas bag and heads towards Lou, the squat, weary-looking club owner who looks more like Ed Asner than Ed Asner. "Strange dream last night," Lou says to Mercy in a heavy Greek accent. "Was in front of a cave. Cave beams pink light, drawing me closer. But I'm scared it will kill me. So, I run screaming. Anything but pink cave. Death before pink cave. What do you think my dream means?"

"Did the cave by chance have hair around it?" Mercy asks.

Lou looks genuinely surprised that she could know.

"Like all of your dreams, Lou, it means that you're terrified of the female anatomy."

"Huh… something to think on. You want cash or Health Credits?" Mercy gives him side-eye, so he hands her the cash. "Give you some free advice, Mercy. Dark stuff not working. People want upbeat. They work a hard job. Don't want to think about death. Like Colby. He does upbeat. He brings covers. That's why I give him mainstage and thirty-six dollars."

"Colby does puns." Mercy looks to the stage at Colby, with his corny khakis and stripy tucked-in Vineyard Vines.

A gaggle of new people are suddenly in the crowd watching him. "My childhood was rough. I was brought up in a foster home. No, literally, my parents are Pat and Irene Foster. No chance of adoption for this kid!" The crowd erupts with laughter, and even the drunks topple over. Mercy rolls her eyes.

"Do what Colby does," Lou says. "Keep it light—bring covers. Then you get mainstage. But now, fifteen dollars or twenty-five health credits."

"Thanks a bunch, Lou." Mercy pockets the cash and heads out the door.

"You come back. I see future."

"Me too. It's called slow death by starvation."

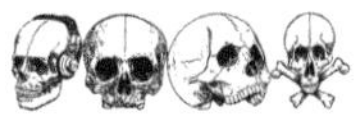

Mercy unlocks her electric bicycle and pedals off down the wet streets until the neon lights turn on and the bike pedals itself. She blasts Gauze, a punk band whose first album I downloaded onto Mercy's phone before I was shipped off to boarding school ten years ago. She stays alert. It's getting more dangerous at night, and you've got to watch out. Word is the Uninsured Resistance are hiding out in subway tunnels and have figured out how to remove the M-Chips from their wrists and temples, but it's leaving big gashes, and the cops aren't fooled by their winter hats and wristbands. When the military comes around they scatter like mice in the alleyways. But some fight back.

Mercy rides past North 44, a nightclub for the Gold Star Insured. Valets park Teslas and wealthy patrons fold hundred-dollar bills into the bouncer's meaty hand. But only a street or two away: filth, grime, poverty—garbage fires light cracked pavement where broken streetlamps falter. Mercy spots a black van parked next to a row of burned-out cars. Two armed officers and a Dogman with a German Shepherd confront a ragged family next to an alley. The family looks hungry and dirty. The father coughs sickly—you can hear the phlegm rattling in his lungs. The German Shepherd sits next to him, and the man looks down at the dog as though just handed a death sentence.

"M-Scan," one of the officers says.

"We paid," the man answers. "It's just not working. We're visiting the Health Embassy in the morning."

"M-Scan," the officer repeats. Now he's got his gun out. The other officer steps forward and points a laser at the man's forehead. A red light, shaped like a triangle, glows from his temple.

"We kept paying for years," the man's wife pleads. "But it's too much. We can't feed our children."

The officers grab him. "Come with us, sir."

"I heard they can visit," the man with the glowing red temple says, desperate.

"They can visit," the officer replies, emotionless.

"He's lying. You're all liars!" The woman shouts. The German Shepherd jumps up and barks viciously. The children shriek and huddle around her, crying.

The man turns to his wife. "We knew this could happen. Do the plan." He then bends down to kiss his children, but the officers carry him away into the van.

The wife and children weep in a tight circle as "The Sick One," as he is now officially labeled, looks out the window forcing a smile until it's too hard to watch and he turns away. The driver sees Mercy watching from the corner and points a blinding flashlight her way. "Move along!" he barks, and she doesn't need to be asked twice.

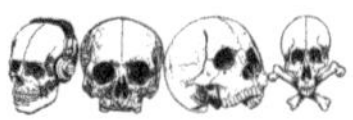

I wish what you just read was the exception to the rule. The Vogovin Virus swept through the country like the plague—million dropped dead in the streets. When it finally subsided, President Phyllis McCabe used fear of its return to create a health care system that no one can afford but the super-rich. She also beefed up the military to enforce it. So now, most of the country goes Uninsured. Getting sick means either going into hiding or disappearing to "The Wellspring," a top secret government-run quarantine the President claims is like Canyon Ranch, but most people suspect is more like Guantanamo Bay. As for the rest of us, we scrounge for government-issued "Health Credits" and pray we'll have enough to see a doctor when we need it most. Or we scratch lottery tickets and hope to get lucky.

And what choice do we have?

Well, my sister Mercy—riding her bicycle into a dingy part of town—is trying to figure that one out.

She's in the South K District, an industrial wasteland even the police avoid. Mercy locks her bike on a filthy pole next to a dark alley, flips her hoodie over her head and darts towards a rusty metal door that looks like it hasn't been open since Prohibition or whenever rusty doors were invented. A slot opens to a giant green eyeball.

"Password?" says the voice inside.

"Whiskey," Mercy says. "And by whiskey, I mean absinthe. And by absinthe, I mean cocaine. And by cocaine, I mean Lady Gaga's ethereal performance in the 2018 remake of A Star Is Born. A timeless love story of eternal beauty and elegance."

The eye stares through the slot again, as if Mercy didn't quite nail that password with the required enthusiasm. But then the door opens anyways.

"You have a straight-up death wish, Mercy?" Gus is Andre-The-Giant-big and totally adorable, at least in Mercy's eyes. He has "Bad Romance" tattooed on the front of his neck, and many other Lady Gaga-inspired tattoos across his massive arms. You sort of have to know Gus to love him, but if you don't, he's probably crazy intimidating. "How are you late every time? Fanny's pissed."

"I had a gig." Mercy shrugs. Gus leans down, cups his enormous hands for Mercy to step onto, as usual. "Love you, Gus," Mercy says, stepping on. "If you weren't into guys, I'd totally let you get some."

"If I weren't into guys I'd already have some," Gus says. "By the way… ew!"

Gus pushes Mercy up towards the ceiling. She removes a slat and pulls herself up into the crawlspace, where she slithers forward twenty-nine feet, past her boss' office and above the Costume Room. She then slides the slat aside and lowers herself into the room and onto a couch below. There are all sorts of crazy get-ups scattered around—superhero outfits, mascot heads, pirate costumes, dominatrix gear too.

Heavy footsteps stomp down the hall. *"Where is she? I'll kill her."* The door swings open. Fanny is mid-fifties, tall and tough-looking with a leathery face from years of hard living in Albuquerque, which is just one reason of many not to live in Albuquerque. She adores a good turquoise brooch, and wears two on her black button-down shirt. Her sneer almost relents enough to betray surprise as she enters the room. "What the hell are you doing here?"

"Insta, for like twenty minutes." Mercy lifts her phone. "Did you know African lungfish can survive out of water for a year?"

"Bullshit. Lucky for you we had a lighting delay."

"We up soon?" Mercy asks.

Fanny shakes it off and pulls up a video on her phone. "It's a standard, with a ninja finish. And a special." She tilts the phone Mercy's way. It's the process they established from the start. Onscreen a frail old man sits on a chair reading from a clipboard. "I do hereby give my full consent to Curated Ends to perform the terms detailed in my Last Will and Testament. I am Uninsured, and I want to end my life outside of The Wellspring. I want to die my way, not theirs." He then gets into the particulars of his special request.

"Lil Nas X?" Mercy asks, aghast.

"Weirdo wants him singing through his death. I think he met his wife in an elevator while 'Montero' was playing."

"So… Brandon?" Mercy perks up.

Fanny sighs. "Your lover boy is already on stage in a pink wig and a diamond choker."

Mercy hands back the phone and follows Fanny down the dark hallway with a giddy smile on her face. Fanny monologues about schedule but Mercy's not even listening—she pulls out a compact to make sure there's nothing in her teeth. And there he is on stage in a curled pink wig, gold bracelets and feathered boa, practicing hip-swaying Lil Nas X dance moves. Brandon makes a handsome Lil Nas X. He's twenty-eight, tall and rangy with an impish grin that Mercy can't quite decipher but thinks is mysterious. She gazes up at him adoringly as Fanny drones on, "... and if we're not out of here and cleaned up within the hour, you know the cops will start snooping around."

The stage is set up like a Valentine's Day suite at a Vegas hotel. Heart-shaped bed with silk sheets, pink walls, furry frills around the mirror. Next to the bed is a tall, beautiful Asian woman dressed in a long silky red dress with matching gloves. She scrolls on her phone, bored.

"New client's a real romantic. Wanted the girl to look like his late wife from Korea who was a pro basketball player. Any idea how hard it was to find a Korean woman over five-nine up for this kind of work?"

"Uh-huh."

"Are you even listening to me, Mercy?"

"Uh-huh."

Brandon walks upstage, smiles at Mercy. "Hey there, Sweetcakes."

Mercy melts. "Hi, Brandon. Nice dance moves."

"What, these?" Brandon spins around, then dances away Lil Nas X-style. Mercy practically swoons.

"He calls everyone Sweetcakes," Fanny says. "Even me until I told him to cut that cheesy shit out."

"I think it's adorable."

The Stage Director, Carlos, walks to the front of the stage with a walkie talkie. "Places everyone. Let's make this dream happen."

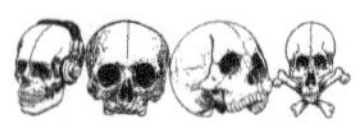

The lights on stage dim and everyone gets in place. The woman in the red silk dress stands next to the heart-shaped bed holding two glasses of champagne. Brandon, a spotlight glimmering off his pink wig stage left, starts singing "Montero" karaoke-style.

Waiting side-stage Mercy unzips her canvas bag and pulls out her uniform: black turtleneck, black gloves, and a black ninja mask. She's dressed entirely in black as she watches the action onstage—an old man sips champagne with the women in the red silk dress, and then the two begin dancing slowly to Brandon's Lil Nas X impression.

"Oh Evelyn, even if this is our last dance, it always feels like the first with you," he says.

"Aw," Mercy says aloud, and Carlos shushes her.

Stage left, Brandon croons and pulls a few dance moves. His eyes are closed—he's genuinely in character. A green light goes on backstage and Carlos taps Mercy on the shoulder. She adjusts her mask and removes one more item from her canvas bag – a long samurai sword, sharp and deadly. Then she goes. Over the sound of the old man's compliments and Brandon's Montero, Mercy leaps onto the stage in a silent somersault, into the splits, and tumble-rolls across the stage without a sound. "Oh, Evelyn. This is perfect. Exactly what I wanted." The old man caresses her butt and smiles. Mercy rises up behind the old man, her sword angled and measured.

"I love you." the man says. "I'll see you soon in heaven."

"I love you too, my dear," the woman replies, extending her gloved hand to his cheek. With one swift stroke Mercy swings her sword. It's a clean cut—the man's head tumbles onto the stage floor, a stunned look left on his face. His body falls the other way, twitching. At once the music turns off and the woman in the red dress grabs a towel, eager to wipe the spray of blood off her. She looks unaffected—business as usual, as if she were wiping pasta sauce splatter off an apron. Brandon has already pulled off his wig. Carlos and Fanny walk onstage to survey the damage—more searching for what needs to be dry-cleaned and what can be hand-washed in the back. Only Mercy is frozen in the position of her kill, sword still angled in place. Her eyes are saucers, mouth hanging open in a trance.

"Fanny, she's doing it again," Carlos says, and Mercy hears him somewhere off in the distance. "Someone wake her up. She's freaking out the talent." Indeed, the Korean woman is eyeing her anxiously.

Brandon walks up to Mercy, grins. "Hey, Sweetcakes. You good?"

But she's not. Instead, my sister Mercy is frozen in a psychosomatic reaction to her kill. A sequence flashes in her mind of the old man she just killed. He's dancing—not with the hired women—but with his late wife, a different, older and more elegant woman. She's telling him that she always loved him and that they will be together soon. She smiles and caresses his face. And then Mercy's vision shifts (as it always does) to a flashback of her own life. She's a little girl in pom-pom hair and pink glasses with an ice cream cone dripping down the sides. She's walking down a city street paces behind our Mom and Dad, who let her get rainbow sprinkles to make her feel better about me (her older brother) being shipped off to boarding school two states away. She's still mad, but she likes to watch our parents together. Mom with those two distinct puffs of curly hair that Mercy emulates and that make her silhouette look like Minnie Mouse. Dad with his big shoulders, balding head, and glasses. They hold hands and nuzzle each other's necks. Mom stumbles a little on an uneven part of the sidewalk and Dad holds her up for support. He says something reassuring to her and kisses her cheek, but Mom coughs sickly and puts a handkerchief to her mouth. Mercy stops behind a garbage can and licks some of the melted ice cream off her wrist, eager for our parents not to see her enjoying every lick. And that's when a black van pulls up and two uniformed men hop out. Mercy crouches down because Dad always told her to stay clear of black vans.

"Insurance Card?" the officer says to our mother.

"No one's sick here, Officer," Dad cuts in, with a relaxed smile. He's always chill; a born peacemaker.

"Yeah, so beat it!" that's Mom—a fierce lioness, claws out in an instant. But she coughs at the end and it's a thick guttural cough. The men grab for her, and Dad's not having any of that. He throws a punch, hits one hard in the face, and there's a struggle, and then a gun goes off. The last thing Mercy sees in her stunned eyes is Mom screaming as the men grab her, and Dad's lifeless body hurled into the van with a thump. And then the van screeches off. Mercy hears Mom yell her name over and over until the van takes a left and the sound fades, and she's alone in the street with melted ice cream all over her hands and wrists.

"Sweetcakes?" Brandon asks again.

Mercy snaps out of it, surprised to see Brandon there. A bit embarrassed. She lowers her sword. "Oh, sorry, just forgot something. Groceries…"

"She's ba-ack," Carlos says.

Brandon grins. "Glad you're with us. Missed you there for a minute."

Mercy pulls off her mask. She's lovelorn again, grinning as Brandon walks off.

"Good work," Fanny says, handing her a thick manila envelope. "You've got dates all next week. What can I say, ninjas are in. You better enjoy it while it lasts. Snipers were all the rage a few months ago." Mercy barely looks at the thick stack of bills inside the envelope—just tucks it away carelessly. Instead she's looking to see if Brandon left already.

"Unbelievable." Fanny rolls her eyes. "Can you please ask him to sleep with you already?"

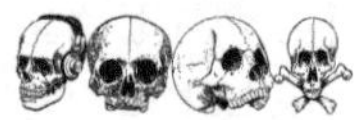

Mercy gets home just past 11 p.m. She parks her bicycle at Cedarville Apartments where "It ain't glamorous, but it's home!" is carved onto the street sign. With nowhere else to go, she's lived here with our grandmother ever since our parents were taken from us. Mercy passes the perpetually broken elevator with the El Vezz gang graffiti and up nine rickety flights to Grandma's door. Four bolt locks and a digital code later and she's in.

"Burglar's here," Mercy announces. "Hide your doily collection."

The apartment is modest but well-kept, the decor decidedly old-lady, including the ornate wooden shoe rack behind-which Mercy hides her canvas bag.

"Mercy? That you, honey?" Nan calls out.

"Who else would it be at this hour?" Nan's friend, Maude, says.

"My Luis?" another voice, Ester, calls out weakly.

"Here she goes again about Luis," Maude says.

"He was almost Aquaman," Ester says.

"Sure. And my Raffi nearly flew to Mars, but Elon Musk doesn't like Persians," Maude says.

Mercy lays groceries down in the kitchen and walks out to the den. There's a walker next to a side table that's awash with Kleenex, medication bottles, and mugs of tea with honey sticks. Nan sits in the middle of her two friends, Maude, who is tall and always wears a mischievous grin, and Ester, who is older, smaller and a bit dazed-looking. "Well if it isn't the Midnight Party Girls. You realize what time it is?"

"He was almost Aquaman," Ester says. "On the TV. Went all the way up to the network chief." As Ester speaks, Nan smiles patiently and Maude rolls her eyes—they've all heard this one a zillion times before. "Did a screen test and they all adored him. Then they found out he was of Columbian origin. 'An Illegal' they called him even though he was born in Minnesota – wouldn't work for the Midwest audience. Passed over for that New Zealand actor with the dimpled chin. But he'll always be my Aquaman…" Ester's voice trails off, a sweet smile on her face.

"We've been waiting for you to watch 60 Minutes." Nan fiddles with the TV remote control like it's a hamster trying to escape. "The DVR hates me."

Mercy takes the remote. "The DVR just needs you to press this."

Onscreen the famous clock ticks, and the ladies adjust their hearing aids as Anderson Cooper speaks in serious tones about a deadly serious issue. "With last year's change in Federal Law, the 'right to die' movement achieved legitimacy in America, allowing The Gold Star Insured to decide when their lives should end with doctor-assisted suicide. But a new crop of illegal businesses for The Uninsured have sprouted up across the country to meet growing demand for people who want to die on their own terms, outside of the government-controlled Wellspring—sometimes in ways that fit their wildest fantasies. Opponents, including President Phyllis McCabe, argue that the unregulated 'curated death' industry is a depraved money-making scheme that takes advantage of the elderly and sick. Supporters, including lawmakers intent on further amending laws on voluntary euthanasia, argue that it's humane to allow people to choose how they end their own lives. With the price of Health Insurance at an all-time high and out of reach for most Americans, the majority of citizens would rather pay to stay out of the unknown of the Wellspring no matter what the alternative."

Mercy's forehead glazes with sweat as the show continues. She grabs the remote control and turns the channel. Kylie Jenner is getting a blowout with her daughters.

"Hey, I was watching that!" Maude complains.

"Sorry, the DVR failed. Yup, you recorded too many shows again," Mercy says. "Oh, geez… now it's erased completely. Sorry, I pressed the thingy and it—"

"Oh, well," Nan says, checking the clock. "I suppose it is getting to be that time."

"I for one don't need an un-invitation," Maude says, packing up her knitting gear. "C'mon Ester. I'll walk you down the hall."

Maude helps Ester up and into her walker. Ester steps forward then stops in front of Mercy. She touches her face with a soft, fragile hand and smiles. "You're a young lady, Mercy. Whole world's ahead of you. Find love. And when you do, nurture it like a garden. Because one day… one day…"

"Thanks, Ester. I understand."

"Good!" Ester. "You've always been a good girl. A good, virtuous girl."

Mercy turns to her grandmother, mortified. "You told them I'm still a virgin?"

Nan shrugs. "They asked, and we all agreed that third base doesn't count. No matter how many times you do it."

"Nan!"

"It will happen, dear. And when it does, wow-ee!" Ester says with a light in her eyes.

Ester and Maude walk out, and Mercy leads Nan to her room. She helps her into the shower, dresses her for bed, injects her medicine, and tucks her in. It's a nightly process they've both come to depend on, when the world feels quiet and safe.

"You sleep tight, darling," Nan says.

"Like if I sleep loose, you'll find a bunch of sailors in my bed?"

"Always joking, my Mercy," Nan chuckles. "I think that one needs a bit of work." She takes Mercy's hand. "If only your mom and dad could see you now. They would be so proud."

"Thanks, Nan. Sleep loose."

Mercy closes the door and stands outside, eavesdropping. Two yawns later and Nan's snoring like a lumberjack.

Mercy checks her phone. There's a text from Fanny: *Up for a double shift? Double $$.* Mercy sighs but then tiptoes to the front door. She grabs her canvas bag once again and slips out into the night.

Chapter 3

You probably have questions. Like, how can my little sister Mercy just kill like that? Doesn't she feel anything when she does it? Is she some kind of psychopath? The easy answer is that she's had so much death around her that maybe she's become numb. Not only our parents' death, but mine too. You see, after the President called for a State Lockdown I went into hiding with a group of people who wanted to fight back. But to truly disappear, I forged my own death certificate and sent a copy to my grandmother's address. I didn't mean to hurt Mercy—I thought I was trying to protect her—but apparently, she didn't speak for two months after that. And when Mercy finally did, it was to ask Grandma to never mention my name again. I was simply suppressed. Holding in all that pain could indeed numb a person, even into killing others.

But I think that answer is a bit too neat. The more likely answer is stranger: My little sister Mercy is b-u-s-y. Maybe even too busy to think about it that much. When she's not working for a curated death company, or pursuing her dreams of becoming a stand-up comedian, she's taking care of Nan. But Mercy also has a day job, and that's all part of the elaborate lie she uses to explain how she and Nan have Health Insurance despite not earning nearly enough money to pay for it.

The big lie: Mercy won a "National Family Health Insurance Lottery" at her Museum job and gets to keep that Health Insurance for as long as she stays employed there. It was the best she could come up with at the time, and Nan stopped asking questions after Mercy presented a letter on stolen Museum letterhead congratulating her. As for Maude and Ester, Mercy simply made regular deposits into their Health Care Accounts, and neither had ever brought it up, maybe hoping it was a rare glitch in the system that worked in their favor.

And what was Mercy's alternative, really? Tell Nan that she kills for a living? Let them all go Uninsured and probably end up in The Wellspring? Not happening. Government-issued Health Credits have been reduced to near-worthless against rising rates, so that's no help. So Mercy kills, and during the day works a museum job that gives her time to write jokes. But also it allows her to hang out with Dee, who (other than me) is basically the coolest person Mercy has ever met.

Today, Dee and Mercy stand in a large dark room before an enormous life-sized Sperm Whale that hangs from invisible ropes, a good replica of New York City's more famous one. They wear matching uniforms of burgundy blazers and gray slacks. Dee, who has spiked hair and the sides of her head shaved bald, somehow makes the lame outfit look cool. The Anthropology Museum bustles with tourists, overwhelmed parents, and families trying to connect over taxidermized African antelopes and Indonesian ritual masks. Tourists walk up to them, but before they can even ask, Dee yawns and says, "Bathrooms are left of the giant squid under the big red sign."

A boy with chocolate ice cream all over his face

runs away from his mother, and the mom calls out, "Grayson, come back here. Don't you run away from your mother!" The boy turns, gives his mother the finger and runs off again. "Grayson! Young man, that is not okay behavior!"

Dee shakes her head. "She should just let him go. He clearly has no sense of self-preservation. In the wild a mother would just, yunno, shepherd off the runt to fend on his own."

"Natural selection," Mercy says. "So, you're saying the vulnerable should just die off? Is that what you hackers are planning when you finally siphon off our identities for good?"

"First of all—shush—there's ears everywhere. And I know that because I hacked the Museum security site last night. You'd be in stiches at the kind of porn the night guard watches." Dee cringes. "What I'm saying is that you've got to get your head on straight or else you're going to end up dead and stuffed like Moby Dick up there. Word is that one beached itself, so was easy to catch. Not even enough sense to save his own life."

Little Grayson and his mother stand before them expectantly. The mom gently nudges her brat, whose snot mingles with the chocolate ice cream staining his face. "Go ahead, Grayson," urges the proud mother. "Ask these girls your question. They work here. It's their job to answer."

"How do whales know where to swim?" the boy asks, and his mom beams as if he's solved the Health Care crisis.

Dee gives Mercy an 'I got this' look. She crouches down with a warm smile. "Well, Grayson, the ocean is a big place and whales can hear amazingly well, so they follow their own kind by sound. Just the way you always follow your mommy when she's calling for you, right?" The boy looks up at his mom, unsure. "But once in a while a whale gets too far away from their mama. And they swim too close to the shore. You know what happens then?" The little boy shrugs. "Well, if a big whale swims too close to the shore he gets crushed by his own weight. Because he's super-big. And he can't do anything. So he just lies there on the beach screaming in agony as his own blubber crushes his bones horrifically until he dies and then gets stuffed and mounted in a museum just like this one."

Mercy gazes up at the whale and then back at Grayson, unable to sit this one out. "Imagine being crushed by your own weight. What goes through a whale's mind when he hits that beach and his nagging wife is like, 'I told you not to eat those last few sea lions, Harold. But do you listen to me?' 'Stop nagging me, Edith, I'm dying over here.' Can you imagine how quickly Weight Watchers would go out of business if humans got crushed by our own weight? You'd approach Cinnabon like you're playing Russian Roulette, 'Okay I'm doing this… no, no! Not yet, okay, let's go, grrrr… I'm terrified of dying!'"

The mother is horrorstruck. The boy's lips quiver and then he runs off. The mom looks at Dee and Mercy like they're monsters before turning her attention back to her fleeing child. "You'll be hearing from your Supervisor about this. Grayson, come back here!"

"I asked you not to practice jokes while we're working," Dee says, unimpressed with Mercy's Cinnabon riff.

"Well, if you'd just come to one of my shows…"

"I'll attend when you're ready for my brutally honest feedback," Dee says.

Mercy looks at her friend a long time before turning away—she's not ready for Dee's truth. "You've probably hacked my webcam and watched my set anyway…"

"What, when you stop stalking your lover boy, Brandon?"

"How do you know about…? Forget it. Pervert." Mercy looks at her friend, both horrified and impressed. "I'm definitely not ready for you to come to my shows."

"Let me know…"

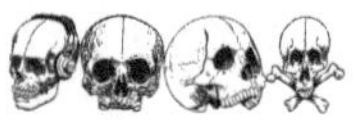

"Death is an awkward social situation," Mercy says, back onstage at the Hilarity Hut. "Anyone here ever died? I mean other than me right now. It's weird, right? Most people don't know how to deal with it. My grandmother Nan knows. When someone dies Nan writes handwritten letters to the loved ones of the deceased. Loving, supportive letters. But sometimes even that goes wrong. Recently, my grandmother wrote a condolence letter to a friend whose husband died. 'Raymond was a wonderful and generous man. He was respected by all who knew him, and he adored you to his very last breath. LOL.' 'Um, LOL?' I asked her. 'Why did you laugh-out-loud sarcastically at the end of this condolence letter? That's cold.' And my grandmother said: 'Oh dear, I thought LOL meant 'Lots of Love.'" Mercy pauses, wrapping the mic wire around her wrist. "Turns out that my dear sweet grandmother had been sending letters to grieving widows all over town laughing-out-loud with sarcasm as she eulogized their dead husbands. 'Henry was a brilliant man, a true intellectual… LOL. Carl was always faithful to you, never once strayed… LOL.' She probably thinks JK means joy and kindness. WTF is probably Why The Frown? LMFAO, I don't know… Let's Make Friends An Omelette?"

Mercy earns mild applause for that one and is

feeling good as she gives up the stage to Colby, who immediately starts punning away to much louder laughter, "If you hook up with someone on jury duty is that considered jury booty?"

Mercy grabs her canvas bag and heads to the exit when her phone buzzes with a text from Fanny: *Got an early one. Can u get here soon-ish? Bonus $$ if within the hour.*

Mercy is texting back affirmative when she bumps into a guy holding two drinks. The drinks spill all over his shirt and pants, and he grins, surveying the damage.

"On the bright side, I did ask the bartender for two vodka sodas, hold the glass," he says.

Mercy sees that it's the cute guy from the back booth whose girlfriend is always sticking a phone in his face during her sets. "Sorry. I was just… Let me buy you a new round. And, uh, dry cleaning."

"No worries." He smiles, backing away. "You've already done enough. Besides, I'd rather go stand under a hand dryer for the next ten minutes than listen to Pun-master up there. You actually saved me from a cringe-fest."

Mercy can't hold back a smile on the Colby dis. "Lowest form of comedy," they say at the same time, and their eyes catch.

"I'm Mercy…"

"…Gorrison. I know who you are," he says. "I'm a fan of dark comedy. And few go darker than you at these shows. You're talented."

Mercy blushes. "You may be the only one here who believes that."

Just then Colby says, "Insomnia is getting more prevalent these days. People are up at all hours. Or as Fox News calls it: the Woke Mob is growing!" The blond girl in the back booth howls with screeching, annoying laughter. The guy acknowledges with a wince that the howler is with him.

"She seems sweet," Mercy says.

"I'm actually trying to break it off. But turns out that I'm a huge coward. Any advice?" he asks.

"Tell her in a way that's meaningful to her: send a meme."

"I like that." He laughs. Then he looks down at his shirt. "Well, hand dryer awaits. Wish me luck, Mercy. Oh, and I'm Nick, since you didn't care to ask."

"I was going to," Mercy chuckles. "Let me know how it goes, Nick."

He walks off and Mercy is unable to suppress a smile. C-u-t-e. But she doesn't get distracted. Mercy looks back down at her phone and tries to focus as she re-reads Fanny's text. Fresh kill awaits.

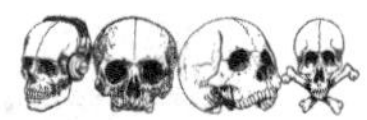

"Whiskey. And by whiskey, I mean absinthe. And by absinthe, I mean cocaine. And by cocaine, I mean Lady Gaga's ethereal performance in the 2018 remake of *A Star Is Born*. A timeless love story of eternal beauty and elegance."

Gus lets Mercy in but stops her before she walks past. "Careful. Dark forces in the house tonight. Code word 'Bradley Cooper' if you need me."

Mercy nods and heads down the hall to Fanny's office, curious about what could earn the moniker 'dark forces' in a place like this. The devil himself? Mercy can smell them before she sees them. Three darkly dressed figures taking up all the space in Fanny's office—they look like a punk tribute band—black trench coats, fingerless gloves and neck tattoos. Corny but dangerous. One is big, maybe 6'6", fat and bearded. He's spinning in his seat and has a hunting knife strapped to his hip as big as a sea bass. A short, thick woman with a mess of tangled green hair and heavy eyeliner lies on the couch with a rifle across her chest. And then leaning against the wall is the Alpha Menace of the group. He's tall and sinewy with a short blond mohawk and acne scars on his neck and cheeks. He's painting what looks like nail polish on the tip of an arrow. They all pay attention to Fanny, who holds court from her desk. They don't seem happy with what's being said. "Maybe next week they'll be something for you. Business is picking up."

"Chin will put on a sumo diaper if they're gay for Japan," the mohawk guy says, whose name is McGroarty. "Kiki can wear a kimono. Right, Kiki?"

Kiki, the one with heavy eyeliner, flips him the bird. The big guy with the beard, who they call Chin, just laughs stupidly. As soon as Mercy arrives at the door she can sense that she's the subject of their bitch-fest. The woman with the heavy eyeliner, Kiki, sits up with her rifle and grins like she can't believe Mercy had the guts to appear. "Well lookie here. It's the greedy ninja girl who's stealing our paychecks."

"Wax on, fuck off," Chin says.

"Enough with the cursing," Fanny says. "You know I don't stand for that shit."

"You're defending this girl?" Kiki asks.

"It's 2034," Mercy says because it's now or never. "Please don't assume my gender."

"She's got jokes!" McGroarty lets out a guffaw. He shoves himself off the wall, puts down his nail polish on Fanny's desk and grips his arrow as he walks towards Mercy. His gray eyes are sinister. "Let me paint a picture for you, k, Ninja Girl? Me and my associates were all ready to get paid tonight. Now Fanny tells us we're no longer needed and that you're the replacement. That won't do. Our time's been wasted. The way I see it, you owe us."

"Not how that works," Mercy says, trying to keep her voice measured.

"Oh? Educate me." He wears a creepy smile, and as he steps closer Mercy can smell his cat-shit breath. She slides a hand into her canvas bag ready to unsheathe her sword if need be. The fat guy, Chin, sees it and grips his hunting knife.

Luckily, Fanny shuts it down. "She'll work when I want her to work." She stands up. They forget what an intimidating figure Fanny can be on her feet. And though McGroarty is still focused on possibly gouging out Mercy's eye with his poison arrow, his attention returns to Fanny.

"As you wish, M'Lady." He bows.

"I wish, Prince Charming. Now go, all of you. I'll have something for you next week, latest. You'll make rent and then some."

McGroarty tips his arrow to his cheek and winks at Mercy. "Careful, you."

The gang walks out and heads to the exit, where Gus puffs up.

"Bunch of psychos," Mercy says to Fanny when they're gone.

"Your colleagues, I'm afraid," Fanny says. "Or as they think of it, your competition. I'll regale you later but right now we've got a live one, and he's getting restless. The guy said he wanted to be shot by a sniper then chickened out, saying, 'what if the bullet doesn't kill me?' So we offered up the Archer, and even that crazy one who guts them with a hunting knife. He wanted a ninja—silent, sudden, sword decapitation. It's a hero scenario—saving a damsel in distress from a mugging. Kill words: 'My hero.' When she says that line, you finish. Got it?" Mercy nods. "Good because we have a hard out on this one and we're already late."

Mercy takes her place backstage, puts on her ninja

uniform, and watches the scenario play out. Brandon is dressed like a thug - hoodie and a ski mask. He's got a gun shoved into the ribs of a curvy redhead with librarian glasses who clutches her purse. "Give me the money." Brandon snarls.

The redhead squeals. "But I don't have any money!"

"Well then you're going to give me something else!" Brandon shouts, and rips at her blouse. Trite, but effective. The old man walks in. He's early-eighties but robust-looking with a thick, veiny neck and big forearms.

"Hey tough guy, knock it off," the old man says, pretty convincingly.

"Beat it, Grandpa. This is between me and her."

"It's between you and me now," the old man says. Brandon raises a switchblade, but with surprising swiftness the man lurches forward and wrestles it out of Brandon's hands. Brandon looks around. "Shit!" He races offstage. The redhead wipes the tears out from under her librarian glasses and turns to the man.

"You saved my life from that terrible man," she says. "How can I ever repay you?" That's Mercy's cue. She leaps onto the stage silently, somersaulting her way behind the man.

"It's payment enough to know you're safe," the man says, and the redhead melts.

"My hero," she says.

Mercy comes up from behind and raises her sword. But just as she's about to swing, she sees her own reflection in the redhead's librarian glasses. The man spins around, a terrified look on his face. He swings at Mercy's face and the fist misses, but his fingernail scratches her eye through the mask hole, and Mercy feels a deep sting. She stays steady on her feet, ducks another punch, and then reels back and swings again. Once. Twice. Three times. It's not pretty. And there's plenty of blood. But it's done.

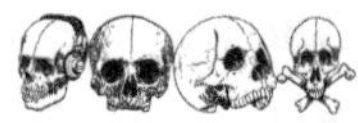

After her usual flashback-freak-out Mercy is back in Fanny's office holding an ice pack to her eye. It stings every time she blinks.

"Goddamnit, I told Carlos to take the lenses out of the glasses before she got onstage. He's so fucking fired!" Fanny paces angrily, fists clenched.

"The old man fought back," Mercy says, stunned. "No one's ever fought back before."

"Human instinct," Fanny says, still fuming. "A scary ninja in your face with a sword. What would you do?"

"This was different. It was in his eyes. Why did he sign up again?"

"Terrible story," Fanny says. "Stage four stomach cancer. Chemo's not working. Health Credits ran out. Didn't have a month."

"No one's that strong after chemo," Mercy says.

Fanny senses Mercy's skepticism and stops pacing. She sits at her desk chair and leans back, which Mercy recognizes as her power pose, but she's not sure why Fanny needs it. And that's when Mercy realizes that she never saw the video.

"You want to see the Death Directive?" Fanny says, reading her mind. Annoyed, Fanny pulls up a file on her computer and turns the screen her way.

In the video the man Mercy just killed sits on a couch, looking frailer than he did in person, with dark bags under his eyes. "I of sound mind and not-so-sound body do agree to choreograph my own death as I would wish it." He has a sweet voice and soft eyes, both of which take Mercy by surprise. "That good enough?" the man asks, looking off-camera to the left.

Another man's voice says, "Yup." And then he begins filling in his personal information.

"Who was he looking at off-camera?" Mercy asks.

"His son," Fanny says. "Look, I'm sorry you got hurt tonight, Mercy. I am. Maybe you need a little time off? I'm sure your grandmother would love to have you home for a while." The mention of Nan reminds Mercy of the cost of her new medication and also the gang of hoods angling to take her place and her money. Fanny pulls out a manila envelope and taps it. "I topped it off with some hazard pay. Should cover the cost of an extra ice pack or two. I'm genuinely sorry this happened tonight, Mercy. And I'm going to make it my business to make sure it never happens again."

Fanny looks at Mercy for a while. She has a way of seeming sincere, especially when money is being exchanged.

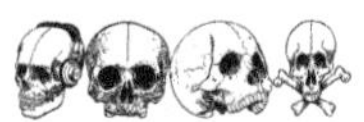

Back at home, Mercy steps in the shower, letting steam fill her nostrils. The image of the old man with the thick neck fighting back keeps coming back to her, especially when the soap stings the cut under her eye. And I understand why. Most of Mercy's kills practically push themselves into her sword. This one swung back. And like everyone who pays attention to the news, my sister Mercy has heard the reports of Uninsured family members pressuring their Sick into curated death as an alternative to the financial ruin that Health Care brings. Right now, she might be wondering if this man was one of those cases? And she was sloppy this time. Forgot to watch the Death Directive beforehand. Those goons distracted her, but that's no excuse. Mercy knows that there's no room for mistakes in the curated death business.

She makes a mental note to ask Fanny harder questions next time when the sound of her phone dings, waking her out of her reverie. Any other night Mercy would leap out of the shower and risk death to read a late-night notification. It could be Lou offering her a mainstage, or a powerful talent agent who'd been hiding in the audience wanting to sign her on! Mercy's mind gets like that in the shower, optimistic to the point of delusion. But tonight, maybe as punishment for her sloppiness at work, she uses Gandhian discipline to dry herself off before grabbing her phone and diving into alerts. It's a DM in Instagram. She swipes so fast she nearly rips off the screen. But it's not Lou or an agent. It's him. The cute guy from the club that Mercy spilled drinks on. Nick's profile pic has him shirtless carrying a puppy. Douche move in my opinion, but apparently not to Mercy, whose knees buckle.

Nick: Was fun literally bumping into you tonight. How about coffee and a pun competition some time? P.S. Your meme idea worked. I'm officially broken up with Instagrrl…

Mercy puts her phone down and squeals. "He understands how to use the word 'literally'!" She then throws on pajamas and runs to her computer and begins the obligatory online stalking. Nick F. Black. What a name. Wonder what the F stands for? Fuckboi? Another shirtless photo on the beach. Hot. Next to a girl in a bikini? "Who's that skank?" Mercy asks the screen as if she's caught her husband with another woman. "Oh, that was like six months ago. He probably dumped her skinny ass."

A chat pops up from Dee on her screen.

Dee: Done with Brandon so soon? Who's this new dude? Cute beach shot.

Mercy: Stop hacking me!

Dee: You make it so easy. Who still uses password as thei. password? Dude is fine tho. Smash!

Mercy closes her computer, grabs her phone and DMs Nick F. Black back.

Mercy: Sounds pun-derful. Saturday night?

Chapter 4

Death is all around her. Skulls, ancient caskets, ritual masks, mummies, and funeral candles from all around the world. The exhibit, "An Exploration of Rituals In Dying," features the Dani tribe from Papua New Guinea, who cut off their fingers as a sacrificial gift to their dead. Mercy is fascinated of course—new material for her set. Dee just keeps shaking her head.

"Goddamn death exhibit," she complains. "This is what I get for telling the Supervisor that his wife put a tracking device on his cellphone, so he better stop making midday booty calls to his side piece."

"You were only trying to help a guy out."

"Exactly." She sighs. "If he puts me in this death room again I'm going to forward his micro-dick pics to his mother-in-law."

That makes Mercy laugh, but she winces at the sting under eye, and touches the soreness.

"You going to tell me what happened to your face yet? And don't give me the line about a bike accident. That's what happens when a fist connects with an eye. You talk back to a heckler?"

Mercy just gazes out at the exhibit. "You ever wonder what really happens when you die?"

"Worms," Dee says.

"Yeah, but what about your soul? What if whatever you believe happens after you die actually happens? Your brain flicks on some survival mechanism that lasts for eternity. Then you'll be eaten by worms for eternity."

"In that case I'll go with Plato."

"If you don't want to talk about it…" Mercy rolls her eyes.

"Plato said that when you die your soul walks through a desert in the hot sun for years and then arrives at a river called The River of Forgetfulness. And your soul drinks from that river because it's parched after the long walk. Once it's done drinking, your soul travels back down to earth into a newborn baby. And however smart that baby is in life is determined by how much your soul drank from the River of Forgetfulness. So we don't actually ever learn anything new. We just remember it from a previous life."

"Wow," Mercy says, genuinely impressed. "You know everything, Dee."

"You're not listening. I don't know anything. I just remember it 'cause my soul wasn't all that thirsty when it arrived at the River of Forgetfulness. Yours on the other hand must have been parched as fuck."

Mercy laughs hard and makes a note to use that bit in her set. Then she goes back to rubbing her swollen eye. But not because it hurts. Because she can't believe who she's seeing enter the Death Exhibit. It's those three psychos from Curated Ends. The massive fat guy with the beard, Chin, Kiki with the eyeliner, and the acne-scarred dude, McGroarty. She can see they're scoping the place out for a burglary, clear as day.

"Check out Bonnie and Clowns over there," Dee says, way ahead of Mercy. She tries to stop Dee from walking over, but Dee's already headed their way.

"Can I tell you something about the exhibit?" she asks the three certified murderers.

They all turn to Dee and give her the up and down. You can tell they're impressed by something about her—her moxie—or maybe how well she rocks that dumb burgundy uniform. Then they spot Mercy slowly emerging behind, and it's almost like they can't believe their eyes either. "Ninja Girl's a museum cop!" Kiki snorts.

"Maybe you'd be more interested in the primate exhibit down the hall?" Dee says, ignoring that.

"Nah, we're in the right place," McGroarty replies. "I heard that ninjas kill themselves with swords when they lose in battle. We have a project for our, uh, adult education class, and were told they have one of those suicide swords up here. Wanting to take a closer look."

"You're confusing ninjas with samurai," Dee says. "To spare themselves the disgrace of being beaten in battle, samurai would commit ritual suicide called *seppuku*. Or *jigai* for women."

"Women samurais?" The fat one bursts out laughing.

"Shut up, Chin." Kiki hits him in the gut.

Dee is unperturbed. "Whereas male samurai would cut open their stomachs, female samurai sliced their own throats. Quicker, more badass way to go if you ask me. Cutting your stomach and lying there moaning is so extra."

McGroarty looks over at Mercy. "Which would you go for, Ninja Girl?"

Mercy doesn't answer, just looks away, and Dee senses her trepidation.

"Exhibit's right down that aisle." Dee points. "Let us know if you have any more questions."

"Danke schoen," McGroarty says, and they walk off.

"Adult Ed, my ass," Dee says, walking back to their post. She pulls out her phone and watches the three of them through the internal camera system. They surround the samurai display's large glass case. Chin looks up at the security cameras stupidly, and Dee takes a screenshot. Kiki taps the glass covering the sword exhibit, testing it for breakage. She looks both ways and Dee snaps another photo. Finally, McGroarty slides brass knuckles onto his fist and is just about to smash the glass right then and there when Dee strides over again. "I'm going to need you to move on." She gives them a look so tough even Chin checks himself.

"Oh, really? Is that what you need?" McGroarty snarls, and it's almost enough to make Mercy rush forward and slice his jugular right then and there.

"It is," Mercy says, finally getting her voice back.

"Ninja Girl speaks!"

"Want me to take her out?" Chin asks McGroarty.

But McGroarty has noticed the cameras, and a sick smile spreads across his face. "Your wish is my command, M'Lady." He takes a deep bow, then nods to the others who follow him out.

Kiki hits Mercy's shoulder as she swaggers by. "We'll be ba-ack."

"Looking forward to it," Dee says, and she watches her phone to make sure they're headed for the exit. Then she turns to Mercy. "What's with them calling you Ninja Girl?"

Mercy shrugs. "Weird, right?"

Dee seems to buy it. At least for now.

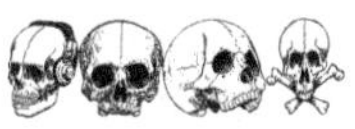

"I don't care how woke language has become, there are still some words that need updating when it comes to women." The crowd at the Hilarity Hut is pretty robust for a Monday, so Mercy is amped. "I'll look past the female equivalent of 'Sir' being 'Madame,' which also means 'owner of a whorehouse.' I'm fine that men get 'Master' while women have 'Mistress,' which is literally a married guy's side chick. Though, even Master is all kinds of racist. Still, those are dated terms. But can anyone here tell me the word used to describe a man who does something incredibly brave? A soldier with a high kill rate or an Olympic athlete who doesn't get caught for steroids?" She looks out to the crowd for a response. Nan insisted she come tonight, so when everyone else averts their eyes Mercy motions to her.

"A hero!" Nan calls out.

"Thank you, Nan. That's my grandmother, ladies and gentlemen. Correct. A hero. But a woman does the exact same thing? We name her after the leading widow-maker of the opioid crisis. Heroine! Joan Of Arc led an army, died stoically, and was sainted. Susan B. Anthony fought against slavery and for workers' rights. Rosa Parks, first lady of civil rights. Oh, them? Heroine. Excuse me? That's a terrible scourge on our nation. There must be some other word. Nope, nope. Heroine. That's what we call 'em. *Heroin* is why my uncle Joey got arrested blowing a dude in Campbell Park. It shouldn't be the name we use for the first Native American woman to walk on the moon. It's like if we called adorable babies 'Crackheads.' Doesn't work!"

The applause for Mercy is louder than usual, and of course Nan is doubled over, making a scene. When Azeem walks on stage his eyebrow arches in a kind of pleasant surprise. "Well, would you look at that? The Dark Lord of comedy, Mercy Gorrison, veering slightly from the subject of death to talk about heroin! Soon she'll be doing comedy about teddy bears and apples—but all the teddy bears are murderers and the apples are poisoned with arsenic! Next up, we have the one, the only, Pun-meister Colby Foster."

Mercy is so filled with adrenaline after a semi-successful set that she motor-mouths to Nan as they leave the club towards a waiting Uber. "That heroin joke? Wrote it this morning! Remember when we were watching that PBS thing? And it killed, Nan, I mean you don't know these Monday crowds—they're deadly." She sounds like a five-year-old at her own birthday party, and doesn't even notice Lou waving money at her in front of the club. She bounces towards him.

"You did good tonight," Lou says, handing Mercy fifteen bucks, which might as well be a million. "Only a little death in your set. Maybe you're ready for mainstage?"

"Don't mess with me, Lou."

"This is your shot. Don't screw me," Lou tells her.

Mercy hugs him. "Lou, you are a lovely man. And God-willing some lonely soul will be into you. But I would never, ever screw you."

"Get outta here!"

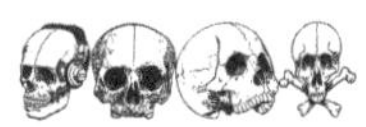

If an above-average set makes Mercy motor-mouth, then an invitation to do her first ever mainstage sends her into hyper-drive. She blathers to Nan through the Uber ride until the driver turns up the radio, and she's still blabbering as she walks Nan up the nine flights of stairs towards the apartment.

"So I say to the guy in the crowd 'what kind of band do you have?' Cause he's clearly a musician, with that hair? And he's like 'it's a post-punk peacenik band,' which is a totally random thing to say. So I'm like, huh, a post-punk peacenik band, may I suggest the name 'Mahatma Blondie'? That just came off the top of my head! I know it's a pun, but that's a good one."

"And the crowd went wild!"

Mercy is still laughing at her own cleverness when they reach the ninth floor and are faced with two uniformed officers. One is a Dogman holding a German Shepherd on a leash, the other is in a standard police uniform. The cop is large, round and ruddy, mid-fifties, with rosacea on his nose and a pronounced frown—his badge says 'Trout.' The Dogman is in the standard uniform of a blue shirt, beige cargo pants and black baseball cap. He's younger and in better shape than the cop. Mercy barely recognizes her new crush Nick F. Black.

"May we help you, officers?" Nan asks, sounding concerned.

"You live on this floor, ma'am?" The cop, Trout, asks.

"In this apartment here with my granddaughter," Nan replies.

Nick avoids Mercy's eyes, but she can tell he knows it's her. His dog stands up and walks over to Nan and sits next to her. "Scan, please," the officer says to Nan.

"Is that what this is about? I thought you're only allowed to do this in the street with those scary black vans?" Nan chuckles.

"Scan."

"Yes, officer, of course." Nan pulls back her cuff to reveal her wrist. When Trout places his scanner, a green triangle glows from the skin.

"Insured?" Trout says, surprised.

Nick finally raises his eyes, relieved.

"We're from the local precinct, ma'am. Nothing to worry about. Just want to ask you a couple of questions. May we come inside?"

"You can ask me anything you want, Officer, but you certainly have not earned an invitation into my home at this hour. Unless you'd like to show me a warrant?" Nan asks.

Trout's face tightens. He eyes his clipboard. "Are you familiar with a business known as 'Curated Ends Incorporated'?"

Hearing her employer's name spoken aloud drains the blood from Mercy's face and makes her fingers tingle. She bites down on her inner cheek until it's about to burst as she remembers that in her canvas bag is everything the cops need to put her away for a very long time—ninja mask, gloves, samurai sword probably with DNA from all of her kills. Nan will be alone and helpless. And without cash flowing, very soon Uninsured as well. She breathes deeply through her nose to calm herself but can see the dog looking her way, suspicious, perhaps smelling fear.

"I've seen a news piece about it," replies Nan. "Sixty Minutes with that handsome devil Anderson Cooper."

"Have you had any contact with that business?" Trout asks.

"You implying that I'm an employee or a client?"

Trout wrinkles his brow and that's when Nick F. Black, the Dogman and Mercy's current crush steps in. "Terribly sorry, ma'am. We didn't mean to imply anything. The police have just been looking into these kinds of businesses and—"

"Not sure why the police need to concern themselves with how people want to end their own lives," Nan cuts in. "And you folks taking sick people off to who knows where, doing who knows what just because they're poor? Can you blame a person for taking control of their own lives? Shameful if you ask me."

"So, you support these illegal businesses?" Trout asks.

"This is still America is it not, Officer Trout, badge number 34977? Am I no longer allowed to speak my opinion?"

Mercy's mouth falls open at how tough Nan still is.

And how she managed to read the cop's badge number in that light only proves she's superhuman.

"Yes, ma'am. You're absolutely right." Nick tries to steady the situation. There's an awkward pause where Trout rebukes Nick with a snarl, and Mercy has time to calm herself. It's getting weird that she hasn't said a word, and she caught Trout taking a gander at her canvas bag.

"Why don't you give us your card and we'll call you if we hear anything," Mercy says. "Of course we want to help however we can."

"Good idea," Nick says, but Trout isn't having an easy end to this exchange. Probably still wondering how someone who lives in this broken-down apartment complex could possibly afford to be Insured.

"What kind of work do you do?" he asks Mercy.

"I'm a—"

"She's a well-known comedienne," Nan proclaims. "A mainstage comedienne."

"Ah, so you've got jokes?" Trout asks, which is what all basic bitches say when Mercy reveals her dreams. "Officer Black here's a big comedy fan."

"She's telling the truth," Nick says. "This is Mercy Gorrison. I've seen her perform, Sir. She's talented."

"Really?" Trout asks, skeptical. He turns to Mercy. "Tell us a joke then."

"She's supposed to clown for you for free?" Nan snaps.

"Well, if I may," Nick cuts in. "She had this one joke where she says, um, I'm going to ruin it but, she asked how come when we talk about struggling artists we never talk about escape artists, since they're the ones who struggle most of all." Nick slips in a wink at Mercy. Both know that he's repeating one of Colby's most groan-inducing puns. Of course, basic bitch Trout bursts out laughing.

"Ha, I love a good dad joke! I'm going to use that." He nudges Nick, and his expression softens as he turns his attention to Nan. "Look, we're sorry to disturb your evening. We've been on the case and came upon the address for this building. So, like my partner said, if you hear anything…" Trout hands Nan a card.

"Of course, Officer," Nan says. She tucks the card away without looking at it.

Trout tips his hat and walks off to the stairs. As Nick passes Mercy with the dog, he mutters. "G'night, Ma'am."

"G'night, Sir," Mercy replies.

When they're gone, Nan pulls out her keys and begins the process of unlocking all four bolt locks. That's when Ester cracks open the door to her apartment. She peeks out into the hall, looking more bewildered than usual.

"That you, Luis?" she asks.

"Just us, Ester. Sorry to wake you," Nan says.

Ester's face falls. "He was almost Aquaman, you know. But he'll always be my Aquaman."

"We know. Goodnight, dear."

"Okay," Ester says, and turns back inside, nodding her head like she just remembered something important.

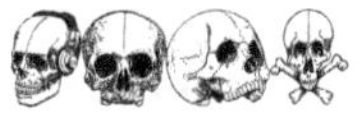

Gus opens the door at Curated Ends. "The one time you're early, we're delayed."

"Where's Fanny?" Mercy asks, all business.

"Woah, Mercy's on a mission—I like it," Gus says. "Office."

Mercy marches over, pissed beyond imagination. Fanny's on the phone, but Mercy doesn't care. "They came to my home, Fanny!" she blurts out. "The cops were at my door asking questions."

Fanny puts a hand up, annoyed. "Let me call you back, 'kay?" She hangs up her call and motions to a chair, but Mercy isn't having it.

"My grandmother was with me," Mercy continues. "She had to answer to the cops about Curated Ends Incorporated. Can you tell me how that happens, Fanny?"

"You tell 'em anything?"

"You would ask that."

"Did you?"

"Of course not," Mercy says. "We're on a list? What in the hell is going on?"

Fanny slumps back in her chair and throws up her hands.

"So, should I just walk myself into jail?!"

"They don't even know what they're looking for," Fanny says.

"Really? Because they seemed pretty specific. Are you fucking with me?"

Fanny flashes her eyes, tiger-like, and Mercy knows things are about to turn. "You watch your language, young lady. And your tone." She stands up—all six-two of her. "If you want to talk, sit. But if you want to curse like a child you can get out of my office and stay out because you're off the goddamn payroll."

Mercy is about to bolt—she's that pissed—but Fanny has her by the wallet and knows it. She collects herself and sits. Fanny turns her computer screen towards her. It's frozen on black and white car cam footage. She presses play and Mercy watches Officer Trout enter a police car and stretch his seat belt over his stomach. He looks into the mirror and picks his nose. Then the back door opens and a German Shepherd hops in. Nick enters the front seat, baseball cap twisted backward. He's carrying two cups of coffee.

"Where're the creamers?" Trout complains.

"You said you want to lose weight, Sir. Those creamers are like donuts."

"Don't get smart with me, Rookie."

Nick hands him a paper bag, and the officer unpeels creamer after creamer into his coffee.

"Where'd you get this?" Mercy asks, but Fanny shushes her.

"Definition of a wild goose chase if you ask me," Trout says. "Bunch of poor old ladies and immigrants at this address. Only one we stop is Insured, so we got no leverage there."

"Want me to write it up as a dead lead, boss?" Nick asks.

"Sarge said to follow it to the end, so we're gonna need to make an arrest in the building eventually. They're gonna need their pound of flesh. But we're no closer on this than when we started." Trout takes a long swig of his cream-filled coffee. "Screw it. Write that floor up as a dead lead. I'll vouch."

"Copy that, Sir."

Officer Trout crumples a piece of paper, the list of addresses on Nan's floor, and shoves it in the trash bag along with his empty creamers. "Fuckin' wild good chase."

Fanny pauses the video. "That was an hour ago."

"Where'd you get that?" Mercy asks.

"A friend in surveillance."

"So, we're in the clear?" Mercy is a bit stunned.

"You watched the same tape I did. He tossed the list, though I'd avoid other floors in your building for a while. And from now on I'm doing all the paperwork by hand. It's too leaky online." Fanny taps a big blank journal to demonstrate. "We've got more friends than you think, Mercy. The cops are behind the times. A lot of people are coming out of the woodwork who believe in what we do on an ethical level, and they're trying to help. They hate everything about the Wellspring. Next thing you know the laws change and we'll be—"

"Legal?"

"Mainstream. But until then, unfortunately, we've got to duck and cover." Fanny softens. She can see Mercy is coming around again. "Let me take you to dinner. Tomorrow night. We can talk some more about it. Plan a bit."

"I can't," Mercy says, eyes downcast.

"Not good business. When your boss offers to buy you an apology meal, you should accept."

"I've got a gig," Mercy says, shyly. "Mainstage."

Fanny smiles and slaps the desk. "Well, look at you. Mrs. soon-to-be-too-big-for-this-popsicle-stand. Listen, I know it's been a bad week. First that screw up with librarian glasses, now this. But I'm telling you, I've got it handled. You and Nanette are safe. You have my word."

"How did you know my grandmother's name?" Mercy asks.

"Huh?"

"I mean, I've told you about her, but how did you know her name?"

Fanny taps the computer screen. "The cops. They say it in the surveillance tape. Nanette Gorrison?"

"Right." Mercy winces.

"Jesus, Mercy. You've got to learn to trust me."

Chapter 5

Hairbrushes make great microphones, and my sister Mercy is trying out new opening bits in the bathroom mirror in preparation for her first mainstage. "How's everyone doing tonight?" she asks the bristles. "Because I actually care. The way you care for someone who accidentally ate all of the hash brownies. Like 'How are you doing tonight?' Checking if you're just high or if I need to rush you to the hospital to get your stomach pumped." She laughs to herself. I remember baby Mercy doing the same thing with a rubber duckie during bath time. Even as a moody kid, I couldn't help but laugh at her babbling monologues. "Nah, that's terrible," Mercy goes on. "Maybe start with Good Evening, mwahaha… Yeah, like a Dracula—Good evening mwahaha—but then what?" She's gets out of the shower and is applying moisturizer (a big-time comedy scout needs to see that young fresh face) when her phone buzzes. Dogman Nick F. Black has slid back into her DMs.

Nick: I've had more awkward first dates, but that was… different. Can I entice you to something less formal?

Mercy decides to reply because she'd rather stop the bleeding.

Mercy: I don't date Dogmen.

Then she closes the app, but he buzzes back before she can even swipe.

Nick: We prefer 'Health Pet Therapists.' Either way, I'm not sensing you see the cop thing as sexy? What if I let you put on the flashy lights in the police car? The woot-woot lights? Whaddya say, Saturday night? Woot-woot!

Mercy closes the app again. No way. But she can feel herself caving. "Damnit."

Mercy: The woo-woot lights can be turned on from the backseat? Cause it seemed like you and that cop were ready to throw away the key.

Nick: I'm not that kind of gal, at least not on first arrest... Look, I'm genuinely sorry for what happened at your apartment. I owe you and your grandmother a serious apology. And if I was especially weird, it's because I got nervous seeing you. I never get nervous in front of a crush.

Crap, now Mercy's back in.

Mercy: Aw, I'm a crush? That's sweet/pathetic.

Nick: Saturday night. Give a lonely Health Pet Specialist with his tail between his legs a chance? If you don't have a fantastic time you can report my badge.

Mercy thinks about it for a while and despite herself leaves the door open.

Mercy: Probably not.

She closes the app, then gets dressed. It's the classic Hollywood-wannabe uniform: black jeans, black t-shirt and Converse. She laces up and throws on a hoodie.

"Leaving so early?" Nan asks. "Show's not 'till ten."

"Lou makes you wash dishes as initiation for your first night as a mainstager," Mercy replies. "He's a jerk like that. I'll see you there."

"Break a leg, Sweetheart."

Mercy grabs her canvas bag from under the shoe rack and is out the door.

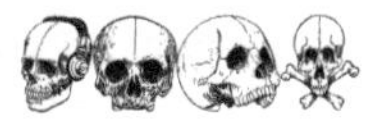

On the street Mercy spots more black vans than usual but that doesn't concern her. Tonight's her big night and they can do whatever nefariousness they want so long as they don't get between her and that stage. She jumps on her bike and drives by The Hilarity Hut just to see her name on the awning, but then rolls right past the club and its fictitious dirty dishes. She rides until she's at that familiar dirty alley, and arrives at the heavy metal door where Gus welcomes her in. Minutes later Mercy is back in her ninja outfit backstage. If tonight's mainstage goes as planned this might be one of her last kills. She's trying to stay focused; her mind needs to be on the set. She looks over her joke sheet, committing it to memory even as she pulls out her sword.

"Almost time," Carlos whispers.

Mercy gives thumbs up and is back on her joke sheet when she gets a text.

Nan: Love you, darling. So very proud of you tonight. Drink in every second. LOL.

Mercy texts back: *Washing dishes… I LOL u 2. Vry mch.*

Just then the green light goes on and Carlos gives Mercy the shoulder tap. She puts on her mask and heads onstage. She's feeling especially creative, so her somersault lands in the classic Spiderman pose. The stage is darkly lit and mellow. There's a couple of old sofa chairs set up in front of an ancient TV set with antenna sticking out in a V. Some old black and white show is on. As Mercy moves closer, she sees a big hand wearing a green glove gently holding a much smaller, frailer hand. The sofa chairs are familiar—old, brown and unstylish like the ones in Nan's apartment. And on the side table is a cup of tea with a honey stick poking out. Mercy's pulse quickens but she doesn't know exactly why. In one of the chairs sits Brandon. He's wearing green tights, an orange chest piece, green gloves—a trident lays across his lap. It's an old-style Aquaman costume. Next to him, Ester sits in the adjoining sofa chair staring adoringly at Brandon. There's a glint in her eye that Mercy has never seen before—a total joy and adoration.

"My Luis. I always waited for you," she says. "You were always my Aquaman."

"Gracias, Ester. Mi amor," Brandon replies.

Mercy touches her sword—it's time—but she can't do it. No way in fucking hell. How did Ester even get involved in this? Mercy thinks back to Nick and Officer Trout's visit and realizes that it was probably her address on the list, not Nan's. Mercy lowers her sword and is about to walk offstage—call the whole thing off and bitch Fanny out—when she hears Gus yell from the back. "Cops in the alley. We're found!"

Mercy sees Fanny running with her computer and a box of files towards the back exit. Carlos follows her with an armful of costumes. Mercy looks back down—Brandon in his Aquaman costume gives her a desperate, pleading look. Ester is still gazing at him, so in love, so peacefully unaware of what's happening; still unaware that Mercy is a killer. But Brandon starts to panic, and Ester's trance will soon break. She will soon be part of all this darkness and despair. Mercy grips her sword, but it trembles in her hand.

"They've got a battering ram!" Gus shouts out. He's running to the back as well, waving to Mercy. "Time to roll."

Mercy grips her sword but can't move her arm, and that's when Brandon shoots up and grabs it. While Mercy watches on as if in a dream, he pulls back and thrusts the sword through the back of the sofa chair. It rips through the fabric and stabs into Ester's fragile body. Ester arches with the force, and Mercy hears a soft grunt as the blade pierces her heart. Ester quickly goes limp.

"Finally!" Brandon says. He releases the sword and runs offstage towards the back exit.

There's a loud bang at the door. Like a bomb. But Mercy is frozen. She sees Ester's apartment and on the couch is Luis—handsome with dark, wavy hair and a kiss curl. They watch TV and Luis is onscreen as Aquaman saving a young woman, who looks like a young Ester. "My hero," she's saying. The couple hold hands joyfully, peacefully, so in love. And then Mercy is back with her ice cream cone and parents and the black van, Dad's lifeless body, Mom's screaming.

The front door of Curated Ends blasts off its hinges and Mercy snaps out of it. Cops in full SWAT gear rush in, pointing guns with red lasers in every direction. Mercy tucks her sword away in her canvas bag and slings it over her shoulder. She leaps up, grabs onto the rafters above the stage, and swings herself onto a thick metal beam. When the cops reach the stage, now with barking dogs, Mercy lies motionless, just breathing adrenaline through her nose. She peeks down and watches them survey the stage. Ester's bloody, lifeless body, the choreographed mess of her death. A mystery of creepy nostalgia and blood. When one officer calls the others to another room, Mercy squirms along the beam towards a small window. She manages to crack it open, slips through, and as flashlights turn up her way, she jumps out into the alley below. Mercy lands hard right in front of a cop car but it's abandoned. She slinks around the vehicle, unpeels her mask and gloves, and throws them into her canvas bag. On her electric bike, she races down the street. Red and blue lights illuminate her as she drives away. Cop cars with sirens blaring slow down next to her but Mercy pretends to rock out to music, so they drive on. At a nearby alley, Mercy ditches her canvas bag in a garbage can lit with flames. The mask, gloves, bloody sword, the whole thing will melt away eventually, she hopes. "That didn't happen!" She rage-screams into her armpit. "THAT DIDN'T HAPPEN!" It couldn't have happened. But it did. Every terrible second of it.

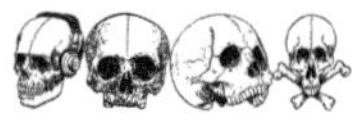

Mercy jumps back on her electric bicycle and turns off the motor so that she can work out some of her adrenaline on the pedals. She arrives at The Hilarity Hut and parks by the back-alley door so that no one will see her in this state. She enters and sneaks into the greenroom, with its broken couch and stale coffee, and tries to compose herself, but time speeds and shakes. The clock on the wall spins. She needs to be there to solidify her alibi, but she also needs to be there for herself. This is her big night—her escape from killing, her path to comedy stardom. She pulls out her joke sheet, and there's dried blood on it and that triggers another tailspin of screaming into her pits. Her hands shake as she goes over the blurry lines of text and her stomach flips. She falls to the floor and crawls to a paper basket filled with empty cigarette packs and setlists from past comedians. Her stomach releases. She's vomiting stomach lining when Lou enters.

He pinches his nose. "You eat baba ghanoush again?"

"Sorry, Lou. Just nerves."

"Five minutes," he says. "Get it together, Mercy. This is your chance."

"I got it, Lou. Just need a sec."

Lou closes the door with a loud sigh and Mercy continues to throw up. She can hear Azeem warming up the crowd, buying her time in front of what sounds like a packed house. "And that's why I'll never use the Pete Davidson voice on my GPS again!"

And then she hears it: "Our next comic is a regular at the club. You may have seen her before, but probably definitely not. This is her first mainstage evaa, put 'em together for the Dark Lord of comedy herself, Mercyyyyyy Gooooorrison!"

Mercy's name rings out through the thick soup of a bad dream. Her body shoots up like a puppet on strings, and adrenaline carries her out of the green room and towards the stage. She pulls back the curtain and the spotlight is impossibly bright—it blinds her as she steps forward. She's a sweaty, pukey mess but Azeem doesn't seem to notice. He gives a fist bump and says, "Go kill." But sound is a vacuum, echoing, awful.

Mercy approaches the mic and it screeches feedback, evoking a bus crash or a factory accident. Her fingertips tingle—a river of sweat flows down her back. She squints through the light and sees a packed crowd that appears as a frowning jury—one by one, giving thumbs down to the hooded executioner. "That didn't happen," she mutters to herself, but the crowd hears it. "Oh… hey," she says finally finding purpose. The audience stares back at her, ready for whatever this is. "Hello, microphone. Hello, crowd." It's not the opening she planned for, but not horrible. Sort of meta. She stares at the microphone as if she's not sure what it is—a bottle of hot sauce or a sleeping squirrel. The crowd chuckles nervously. "Yes, Hello, Ms. Microphone. You've been working out? You look good."

"Speak into it!" a heckler from the crowd says.

"Right. That's my job," Mercy says. "I say things, you laugh."

"That's the arrangement," the heckler retorts, and the crowd laughs.

Light settles, and Mercy spots Lou in the back watching on. Nan is at a table with Dee, and they both smile expectantly. Mercy is still getting the benefit of the doubt. But she's completely blanked on her set and realizes that she left the blood-stained joke sheet back in the green room, so she just pushes out something that's probably not even hers: "So, uh… anyone notice that your Netflix queue is kind of the person you are, but what you actually watch is the person you want to be… Oh, crud… I got that backwards." She smiles. Honest mistake. "Your queue is who you want to be, like a documentary about feminist activism in Burma but then you watch like… some dumb movie… um, I had one… uh, Die Hard 6."

"You're the one who's dying hard," a second heckler shouts, now emboldened.

"This is the Nakatomi Plaza of comedy?" Mercy replies. That gets a chuckle. "Uh, yippee-ki-yay."

"Clever!" a female voice says from the back. Mercy is pretty sure that it's Nick's ex-girlfriend since it came from a face lit up by a glowing screen. Mercy's hands are so sweaty that the microphone momentarily slides from her wrist. She tries to reposition it, but it gets away from her and whacks against the mic stand. When Mercy leans forward to reposition it, her hair catches on the clip. There are some cackles from the crowd as she rips it away—they think she's trying physical comedy.

Dee is looking down at her phone now, shaking her head like 'I told you not to invite me if you're not ready.' Mercy feels the sourness in her stomach coming back up and she knows this won't end well. She'll be damned if she's going to be that nervous comic who pukes on stage. "I feel a little under the weather. And I don't want to throw up and end up some internet meme about how when you think it's Friday but it's only Tuesday… So, uh, I'm gonna go," she says to the crowd. She gives Lou an apologetic glance, shakes her head, and steadies the mic.

"So soon?" Nick's Ex calls out.

As Mercy turns to leave, she catches a glance of Nan's face for some kind of reassurance, which she gives her, pityingly. Mercy can barely see through the sweat falling into her eyes, but she makes it past Azeem and down the shaky hallway. She pushes through the back door and into the thick night air just in time to throw up again into an overfilled recycling bin. Some of her own vomit splashes on her, but even worse, she can still hear the hallway speakers from the stage and so is subjected to the torture of hearing Azeem apologize for her Titanic disaster on stage.

"Let's give a big hand for Mercy Gorrison. Apparently, a minimalist comic. Part of the Twitter generation. Only a hundred and forty characters in her set. Okey dokey, let's bring up our next comic, the inimitable Pun King, Colby Foster!"

Mercy readies to puke more when a beam of light hits the side of her face. She's hoping it's not Dee since she can't handle her disappointment after such a colossal failure. Nan might be even worse. She knows Mercy so well that she might already know what happened to Ester. But when Mercy looks up, she sees Lou standing in the doorframe next to two men in dark suits.

"Hey, kid," Lou says.

"I'm sorry, Lou. I'm a loser. You should never have given me a chance."

"It wasn't great, I'll admit. But it's not that." He has a sad expression on his face. "These men are from the police—they want to ask you some questions."

So this is how it ends?

Mercy should have known. She wipes the sides of her mouth and checks her shirt for stains. She's seen pukey mugshots before and doesn't want to be immortalized that way. She thinks about making a run for it down the alley, but her legs are Jell-O—wouldn't make it two steps before they'd tackle her. So, Mercy just stands up as tall as she can, turns to them, and extends her wrists for handcuffs.

Chapter 6

The interrogation room is small and airless. Gray walls, metal chairs and a desk, and a two-way mirror right out of Homeland. Across from Mercy is Officer Trout, with rosacea and his deep frown. He has a bandage on his neck that was probably a shaving cut but the bandage is big enough to be from a stabbing wound. Drama queen. "This can go one of two ways," Trout says. "I'd rather do it the easy way and not waste too much time?"

"Yes, officer," Mercy says, head bowed.

"Good." He gets out his notepad. "So, this Curated Ends Incorporated. When did you first hear about it?"

"Not sure I understand what that has to do with anything?"

"The deceased. Ester Gutiérrez. Did she speak to you about Curated Ends?"

"Not that I remember."

"So she gave you no indication? Not even a hint that she was… suicidal?"

"I mean, she complained about her hip," Mercy says.

"Bad hip." Trout jots that down.

"She went skiing in Quebec once, many years ago. Hip has bothered her ever since. But Ester was pretty religious. She talked about God's plan. She did miss her late husband a lot."

"Yes. A Mr. Luis Gutiérrez?" Trout keeps writing. "Mr. Gutierrez was a janitor at the local public school. The salary of a high school janitor doesn't leave much for extras, I don't imagine?"

"Sounds like you're judging a dead man," Mercy says.

"My uncle was a janitor in the public system," Trout replies. "Was a struggle for him to pay for health insurance. And yet Mr. Gutiérrez was fully Insured and so was Ms. Gutiérrez. In fact, according to her records she never lapsed in paying her Insurance, even after Mr. Gutiérrez passed."

"He had acting jobs. Commercials. Ester said he hit the jackpot with a Volvo ad that went national."

"So, residuals from TV?"

"Yup."

"What's puzzling to me," Trout says, touching the bandage on his neck. "Most people who use these curated death services don't have the option to be in the hospital with a doctor where it can all be more controlled. They're Uninsured. So why do you think Ester would opt for this?"

"Would you want to be cooped up in some hospice until some kid with an online medical degree gives you a lethal injection?"

Trout sighs. "What about the Aquaman costume? It had blood on it, so it must have been part of the uh… curation."

"Ester swore up and down that Luis would have been cast as Aquaman 'if it hadn't been for that racist network executive,'" Mercy imitates Ester when she says this, and then laughs, a nice release.

The cop looks at Mercy like she's a little crazy. Mercy starts to tear up, and Trout hands her tissues.

"I understand this is hard for you. I just want to make it clear that what happened tonight was murder in the legal sense. So, if you can think of anyone Ms. Gutiérrez might have been in contact with— anyone who might have influenced her to do this? That would be helpful."

"Of course."

Out in the hall, Nan and Maude are waiting there for Mercy, frowns even more pronounced than Trouts'.

"She's been very helpful." Trout says, then turns to Mercy. "And sorry that I had to interrupt your, uh, art performance." The mention of Mercy's career-ending mainstage makes her cringe deeply. "Good thing is that we have some strong leads on who did this. The Aquaman costume will likely yield DNA, which will help. You can be sure we'll find the people involved in your friend's death. And we'll bring them to justice."

"Is it really justice to punish the people who helped an old gal get exactly what she wanted?" Maude asks Trout.

"It's the law, ma'am."

"Yeah, for the poor," Maude mutters.

Trout hands Nan a card. "If you remember anything, I'm always available."

"Thanks. Means a lot." Nan takes the card and drops it into her purse.

The three of them head towards the exit.

"Well, that was some hot bullshit," Maude she says, loud enough for Trout to hear loud and clear.

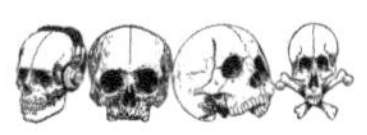

Rows of padded chairs are set up on a grassy hill in front of a podium with flowers, and a walnut casket. Ester's grown children stand near the front, weeping as if their own hearts have been ripped from their chests.

Loud and dramatic like in a telenovela. Indeed, one of them takes a selfie next to the casket. Mercy, Nan, and Maude sit near the back. Dee joins them, dressed in an all-black tux.

"Are we sitting back here to give the phonies from Ester's extended family room at the front?" Dee asks, having somehow read everyone's mind.

"I like her already," Maude says, and gives Dee a squeeze on her arm. "You'll sit next to me, dear."

They start whispering to each other like old friends, and Mercy is glad to not have to talk. Even though Brandon had the courage to do the deed, Mercy feels all the shame of being a murderer attending the funeral of her victim. Her hands tremble the same way they did when she was holding the sword that impaled Ester, and she swears people are stealing glances at her, whispering. *'That's her. Too chicken-shit to give Ester what she wanted yet too evil to save her.'* Part of me wishes I could sit there with her—hold her hand for reassurance. But I'd just be another ghost rattling in Mercy's head.

Once the priest arrives and everyone takes their seat, it's just another sad funeral. Sun glimmers down through the leaves of swaying oak trees. When the casket is lowered into the ground Mercy scans the mourners, maybe looking for someone that reminds her of Ester. And that's when she sees Nick F. Black. He's off to the side, wearing a dark suit and holding up a sun umbrella for a stylish elderly woman standing next to him. That woman balls her eyes out and then blows her nose into a handkerchief and leans up against Nick for comfort. Nick hugs her awkwardly and when she pulls away, she leaves some snot on his lapel. Mercy snickers as Nick dabs the snot while still holding the woman's sun umbrella in place.

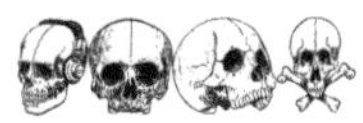

After the service, mourners gather for finger food and coffee in a bright sanctuary with stained glass. There's a large photo of Ester on an easel, younger and happy, set next to a mountain of flowers. Mercy, Nan and Maude are beset by guilty relatives who thank them for "taking care" of Ester, and claiming they were always hoping to visit "if they only had the time."

"Funny thing," Maude made sure to reply to the ones she knew never even called. "Ester never mentioned you at all."

Mercy spots Nick at the buffet table, making a meal out of tiny egg salad sandwiches. She creeps up from behind. "You here for the autopsy report, or to strip search the mourners?" When Nick turns around with a pained look on his face, Mercy realizes how crass that was. "Sorry, that was stupid."

"I heard about Ms. Gutiérrez at the precinct," Nick says. "Just wanted to say I'm sorry. But you're right. I shouldn't have come. I feel like a jerk."

"No, it's sweet," Mercy says. "You're actually doing me a favor. If I stand here with you, the old ladies might stop asking me when I'm going to get married. One of them tried to pawn me off to her fifty-three-year-old son who's a periodontist from Wisconsin."

"So, I'm your funeral husband?" Nick asks.

"Is there any other kind?"

Nick grins. "From the eulogy Ester sounded like an amazing person—"

"God, I hate funerals," Mercy cuts him off. "It's like a game where everyone's gathered because of death but no one dares mention it by name. So sorry to hear of Ester's *passing*. It's not a gallstone. She's in a *better place now*. Like, how is that a better place?"

"Yeah, she didn't move to Philadelphia," Nick says.

"Did you just quote W. C. Fields? How old are you anyways?"

"Ancient."

"Take me out of here Nick Black," Mercy finds herself saying.

"Now?"

"We were supposed to go on a date tonight anyway, weren't we?" Mercy asks.

"I thought you said—"

"Read between the line, dumbass."

Mercy walks off, leaving Nick totally confused. She kisses Nan and Maude goodbye, tells them her escape plan. Then she walks over to Nick, takes his hand and leads him out.

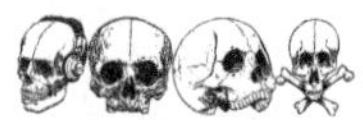

I won't go into the groan-inducing particulars of how my younger sister ended up losing her virginity on the day of Ester's funeral. Her "Prison Confession Tape" goes into excruciating detail, and it was hard for me to transcribe without gagging.

Mercy and Nick F. Black left the funeral together. They went to a tacky hipster bar and did axe throwing while Mercy tried to hide that she had the skills of a trained killer and could split Nick's axe in half with her eyes closed. Then, like a couple of amateurs they both did Jaeger shots, which naturally led to them making out in an elevator, and then stumbling into his apartment where Mercy swears she was only going to go to make out, but then she met Ethelfled, Nick's impossibly old three-legged dog with glaucoma. When the dog's tail wagged, her entire body shook. Mercy lay drunkenly on Nick's kitchen floor, letting the adorable three-legged dog smother her with kisses. And that's where I'll pick up Mercy's story because her Prison Confession Tape specifically asks, "Please don't skip this part because it's the most romantic thing that ever happened to me." So, out of respect for my sister, here they are in Nick's apartment, and my little sister Mercy is lying drunk on his kitchen floor.

"Are you for real?" Mercy asks, slurring a bit. "A hot cop with a sense of humor and a three-legged dog named Ethelfled? If you didn't suck at throwing axes, I'd think I was being Punk'd."

Nick takes Mercy's hand and pulls her off the floor, Ethelfled getting in one last lick. "And you my lady are a sexy, wildly talented comedian who takes care of her grandmother and is weirdly good at axe throwing. What else do I need to know?"

They kiss and it's so amazing that Mercy loses herself. "I'm a virgin!" she blurts out. "I've never, uh, gone all the way. So, if this is going to happen—Is this going to happen? Because I was just going to make out with you, maybe go to the second, or, okay third base and then think of an excuse why I had to go. But then I met your three-legged dog Ethelfled and your apartment smells like vanilla and figs, and…" Nick's eye contact is off. She's screwed everything up and she knows it. "You don't want the responsibility? It's too much. I knew it. Dammit, Mercy," she scolds herself.

"No. No, it's just... I've never been with a virgin before," Nick says, then a smile creeps onto his face. "I'm a virgin to virgins. So, I'm no good at math but that makes three virgins in one bed. A threesome. A virgin threesome. My first time too." He kisses Mercy again and then picks her up off the ground into his arms. "Let's all get deflowered together."

Okay, I'm skipping the part where Mercy describes "a display of virgin passion that may have cleared up Ethelfled's glaucoma." And I'm definitely skipping the part where she talks about using Nick as a "flesh trampoline." Mercy can write jokes but she's terrible at smut, so I'll pick up after it's *finally* over:

"That was... wow," Mercy says, sheets twisted around her body ("*...like a boa constrictor made of combed Egyptian cotton...*"). They snuggle in bed, and Ethelfled rubs up against Mercy's hand.

"Wow, she really likes you," Nick says. "You ever consider a dog?"

"You want a dog in a nine-floor walkup? You saw where I live."

"I did see where you live." Nick says. "I was thinking about that day. It must have been Ms. Gutiérrez. That's why your address was on the list."

"Makes sense," Mercy tightens up.

"I feel like such an idiot. I could have stopped it," he says.

"Oh, big manly man's gonna stop a death even though it's what a woman wants?"

"Not all of them do," Nick says. "There's reports that some who go to curated services get pressured by family who want inheritances, which get more complicated if they end up in the Wellspring."

Mention of the Wellspring gets Mercy agitated. She thinks back to that older man with the thick neck who had genuine fear in his eyes when Mercy faced him with her sword.

Nick senses her agitation and slaps his forehead. "Sorry. What an idiot. Your friend dies and I'm spouting conspiracy theories. I'll shut the fuck up."

"How would you stop them? When people don't really want to die."

"Need to get ahead of one—then blow it all open—who made it happen, who hid it, how high does this go up? These people are killers."

Adrenaline makes Mercy stand up suddenly and

she can't stop herself. She's gathering her clothes.

"Where are you going?" Nick asks.

Mercy tries to act casual. "I've seen enough rom-coms to know that you don't stay over on the first night."

"Crap—I screwed up. Idiot!"

"Tonight was special, Nick F. Black. My first threesome. I'll never forget it."

"What are you doing tomorrow morning for breakfast?"

"DM me," Mercy says then bends down to pet the dog. "Bye, sweet, sweet Ethelfled. Stay wonderful."

Nick watches a bit befuddled as Mercy gets back in her funeral dress and prepares for her walk of shame. "Can I at least drive you home?"

"Already got an Uber," Mercy says on her way out. "Toodle-oo."

Out into the hall, Mercy is finally able to breathe again, but her mind is roiling. It was a clumsy exit—he must suspect something, he's a cop after all—probably saw right through her line about rom-coms! Why did she have to throw the axes so well? And what the hell is 'Toodle-oo'?!

But then something even more dramatic occurs to Mercy and a blushing smile spreads across her face. "I'm not a virgin anymore," she proclaims aloud, then skips down the stairs. "This will be my little secret. My sexy little secret!"

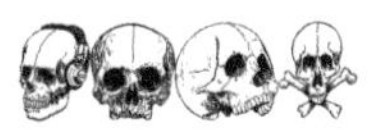

Dee grins. "You nasty little ho."

"What did you call me?" Mercy asks.

"You're wearing eye makeup and perfume."

"So?"

"You had sex last night, didn't you?" Dee asks.

"Jesus Dee, did you hack my watch? You didn't film it? Tell me you didn't."

"First of all, no one on earth wants to see that nasty footage. But I knew you had some sex. The dog cop from the funeral? You're nothing but a horny turncoat. Just admit—you finally got some?"

Mercy can't hold it in. Her smile is too full.

"Deets!" Dee says. "Was he sweet? Was he gentle? Or kinky! He got all Fifty Shades and pulled out wax and feathers? Did you get whipped? Did you whip?"

"He was sweet. We had fun. Honestly, I had no idea you were such a gossip."

"My girl is gone with the wind!" Dee does a full three-sixty turn. "You let me know when you want me to hack him. All I need is basic information and you can read his DMs."

"I don't wanna know."

"Yup, Mercy's in love."

Just then, Mercy's phone vibrates. It's yet another annoying text from Fanny asking her to come back to work. But this one's more specific.

Fanny: Special request. Requires your expertise… and museum access. DON'T IGNORE. Big $$$. Call me!

Mercy puts her phone back without answering. She's deeply pissed at Fanny for what happened with Ester, and even as her first day as a non-virgin, still holds a grudge.

"You're not even going to text him back after he made you a woman?" Dee asks.

"He didn't make me a woman!" Mercy's laughing again when Dee alerts her to a sight that makes her question reality.

"The cast of True Blood returns," Dee says. Of course, her instincts are lightning speed. "They might as well be carrying a sign that says they're robbing the place."

It's the three assholes from Curated again: Chin, Kiki and McGroarty. They've not-so-casually made their way into the Death exhibit for the second time while Mercy and Dee are on duty. They're twitching and looking around like they're about to rob a bank. Or a museum. But why? She watches them walk up to the Samurai exhibit again. Chin fogs up the glass, paints X's and O's like an idiot.

Dee walks over, and again Mercy hesitates to follow, and re-checks her text.

"First sign of trouble, and you bail on me again?" Dee's eyebrow arches in a way that says accompanying her is non-negotiable, so Mercy walks along. The thugs hardly flinch when they approach. "Sir, I'm going to need you to not fog up the glass—you'll trigger the alarm," Dee says to Chin.

"Breath can't trigger an alarm," he replies.

"Have you smelled your breath?" Kiki asks.

"It's heat-sensitive, Sir," Dee says.

McGroarty turns to Dee, sneers. "You a cop or something?"

"Museum curator. Still interested in samurai suicide?"

"Actually," McGroarty takes a menacing step towards Dee. "We're looking for something more specific." He looks at a note crumpled in his hand. "The Temujin Death Sword. It's uh, a Turko-Mongol saber that Genghis Kahn was said to have used. Where's that?"

"That's the one, right there," Dee points. "A priceless artifact. So please, don't fog up the glass."

"Take it out of the display," McGroarty says.

"Sword's staying in the case," Dee replies.

"See, that's the thing—it isn't. But it may not be us that's takes it out of there. It may be your silent friend over there." McGroarty motions to Mercy. "She's the real thief. We're just trying to protect it."

"I'll call security," Mercy says to Dee, lifting her walkie. "These guys are completely off their meds."

"We know Fanny talked to you about using this sword for a job. But that's our job, and our fucking money. And we're not going to let you have it. Understand, Ninja Girl?"

"We've got a seven-o-one on three in exhibit F," Mercy says into the walkie.

McGroarty pulls an arrow out of his shirt. He grabs Dee and presses the tip of it to her neck. "Let's not do that, shall we? I wouldn't want to make a mess of your friend."

Dee freezes in place as McGroarty strengthens his grip. Mercy is already planning McGroarty's death. If she breaks the glass of the display she can probably kill him with a shard. But not before he impales Dee.

McGroarty smiles. "Oh, now Ninja Girl wants to be a hero? Well listen close, hero. You're going to get me that sword, see? By tomorrow. Or both of you are dead."

Mercy lunges forward at lighting-speed and snatches the arrow from McGroarty's hand before he has a chance to stop her. She snaps it over her knee. McGroarty releases Dee and she falls to the ground. Mercy holds out the two jagged edges of the broken arrow, ready to fight to the death with all three of these assholes if that's what it takes, when Security arrives.

"Problem here?" the security guard asks, hand on pistol.

McGroarty winces. "We're just leaving. Aren't we, Ninja Girl?"

"They're just leaving," Mercy repeats.

"I'll escort you out," the Guard says.

The three thugs give Mercy a series of death glares as they walk by and McGroarty reminds her, "Tick

Tock, Ninja Girl."

Mercy helps Dee off the floor, who massages her neck where a poisonous arrow almost impaled her. She looks at Mercy like the world has turned upside down. "You ready to tell me what the fuck is going on?"

Chapter 7

"Anyone noticed how hard it is to fake your own death?" Mercy asks into a microphone. "Hard, right? I find the hardest part about faking my own death is tying a proficient sailor's knot. And if it's hard for regular people, imagine how hard it is for celebrities? They have to deal with internet eulogies. You've seen 'em. The biggest attention-seeking narcissist on your social media feed making a celebrity's deaths entirely about them. Rest in peace Antony Bourdain, the reason I became a chef and winner of Willowdale's spiciest chili contest two years running. #bourdainandme #goingforthreewins. Remembering Toni Morrison today—the reason I became a novella writer and social justice warrior. #amwriting #buymychapbook. If they're truly heartless they post a selfie with the dead celebrity from some book signing like it's evidence they somehow gave the celeb their big break early on. Some periodontist from New Jersey with a dad band called The Well Hung Jury claiming he gave Prince the idea for Purple Rain. If Prince is on some Island in French Polynesia and reads that he'd peel off his fat suit and be like 'screw this. some douchebag going by @guitargoat69 isn't going to sully my decades of hard work. I'm coming back!' Tupac was fine with the hologram concert but when some private school kid named Chason tattoos Thug Life on his abs, Tupac is calling Biggie, 'Pack up the records Biggie, we're going back. Oh, and Biggie, leave behind your Cosby sweaters. I'll explain later...'"

Mercy heads off stage, collects her measly fifteen bucks from Lou, and heads out. The set wasn't great by her standards, but she's rebuilding from nothing. It's part self-torment, part penance. When Lou offers time options for the next show, Mercy chooses the worst, latest spot. If she's a rising phoenix, this is the part when she's covered in ash, hoping her wings aren't permanently damaged. Mercy is unlocking her electric bike when she hears the unmistakable stomp of heavy cowgirl boots approaching.

"Nice set," Fanny says. "I'm hardly in the biz, but isn't a midnight slot on a Tuesday what they call 'paying dues'?"

Mercy climbs onto her bike. "Got to start somewhere."

Fanny steps in front of her and holds onto the handlebars. She's had enough of Mercy's self-pitying and is used to asserting herself. "You've had a month, Mercy. I know it's been hard. But it's time to get back to work."

"No, thanks." Mercy tries to yank herself away.

"You think I don't know what it takes to keep your grandmother Insured? You're not making that kind of cash at the museum."

"None of your business." Mercy meets the eyes of a woman who basically terrifies her. "Use one of your other goons."

"They're too clumsy," Fanny says. "I need you."

"Enough lying, Fanny. You want me to steal a priceless Mongol saber from a museum with a state-of-the-art security system. What, so I can lose my job and go to jail for you? Sorry, I can't think of a single reason why I'd do that."

"The client's rich." Fanny finally averts her eyes like she didn't want to share that information. "Get that sword, yeah, you risk jail. But whoever does get that sword gets the job. And that job means more money than you'd make in years working at the museum."

"I said no."

"A hundred grand, Mercy. For you alone."

"Four hundred," Mercy says.

"Excuse me, what?" Fanny is incredulous.

"You said the client's rich? Four hundred thousand dollars and I'll get the sword and finish Richie Rich. But after that I'm done. Done-done, and you have to agree on that. It's non-negotiable."

"Not possible."

"Those are my terms."

Fanny takes a big deep breath, releases the handlebars.

"Good." Mercy pulls her bicycle away and pedals off, praying it's the last time she sees Fanny ever again.

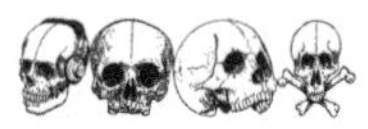

The next morning, my sister Mercy waits outside the hospital for Nan. Guards are on high alert after an incident at a regional hospice where an old lady snuck in with bombs strapped to herself rather than go to The Wellspring, so Mercy isn't allowed to accompany Nan inside. Guards eye her suspiciously, and Dogmen roam the perimeter with their dogs, who sniff, bark, and do the nefarious work of identifying The Sick for their M-Scans. Red you're dead, or whatever the hell happens out there at The Wellspring. President Phyllis McCabe still won't release a sliver of information, and the Speaker of The House is too chicken-shit to bring it up. Once in a while McCabe carts out some old person in front of a camera who swears it's bliss at The Wellspring and The Uninsured are getting the best care and are happier than ever. They tell a sob story about how they were terminal but now are on the mend, it's a miracle, all because of the Wellspring. I personally call a heaping pile of bullshit and would tell the world if I just had some hard evidence, but the Press eats it up. What choice do they have?

Finally, the main doors open and a nurse rolls Nan out in a wheelchair. Mercy helps her into an Uber.

"Sorry I couldn't come in, Nan," Mercy says. "They're extra strict today."

Nan doesn't answer, eyes pointed out the window.

"You feeling okay? If you're woozy you can lie down."

"I'm fine," Nan says, but there's a sternness in her voice that Mercy isn't used to.

She's about to say 'suit yourself,' but Nan straightens up.

"You must think I was born yesterday, huh? Just an old fool who you can lie to?" *Uh-oh.* "After my appointment I went to settle my account, and they showed me my file. I'm not on your Museum Insurance at all. And yet, I've been getting my expensive medical treatments every week. Led right in there like I'm made of money. You want to tell me how that's possible? Well, you don't need to. Dr. Humbley explained that you've been paying cash out-of-pocket for nearly two years. Stand-up comedy must be going well, he said. A fool!"

"Damn it."

"Now tell me, and don't you dare lie. How is it possible that you're paying all that money to this hospital and still buying groceries when I know darn well that what you're making at the museum isn't close to that?"

"Nan..."

"Is it drugs? Did I raise my granddaughter to be a drug dealer?"

"I promise it's not that."

"Then what?!" Nan never raises her voice, so this stuns them both, and even more shocking is that Mercy raises her voice back.

"I won't let you die!" she blurts out, and her voice cracks, which makes her sob a bit. "Not like mom and dad and Theo. I won't be able to live anymore if I lose you." Now Mercy is full-on crying in an Uber, tears just rolling down her face. And I could cry too. It's the first time Mercy has spoken my name since she saw my phony death certificate. "I can't."

Nan settles herself, gets quiet, which is almost as scary as hearing her yell. But she was affected by hearing my name as well. Her eyes get wet. She rests a hand on Mercy's hand. "When you love someone there are things you're willing to turn a blind eye to because you trust them. I love you deeply, Mercy, and I know you're trying. But this illness is not only eating me up, it's consuming you too. You should be out there living your dreams, not getting in trouble for medical payments. Ester chose the way she died. Maybe it's time I go that way too."

"Pull over," Mercy tells the Uber driver.

"Extra stops cost more," the driver says.

"Now." The car stops on the side of the road. Mercy faces forward, trying not to crack. Her pulse speeds, but her voice is measured and intense. "You can never do that. Promise me you'll never ever do that, Nan."

"You have your whole life ahead of you, Mercy, and I'm old—"

"Promise me, Nan. Right now!"

Nan takes a deep breath, looks at her hands. "Okay,

I promise you. But I'm not afraid to die, Mercy. I believe God has a plan for me. I believe in that process."

Mercy breathes a sigh of relief as tears fall down her cheek. "Love you, Nan."

"Good," she says. "Because I love you to my last breath. But when that day comes I want you to promise that you'll be free with your life."

"Nan?" Mercy say, wiping my face of tears. "Can we please not talk about this again for a little while?"

"A little while."

Mercy tells the driver he can go again. He pulls off from the curb and drives off towards home.

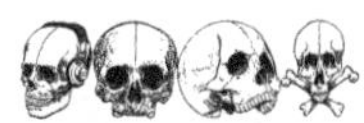

"Why are you blowing up my phone?" Dee asks, when she sees Mercy standing outside the Museum.

"I didn't even call you," Mercy says.

"Not technically, but I created a program that shows me if you were looking at my contact. So you were thinking about calling me."

"That exists?"

"Let me guess. That cop got you pregnant and now you need my hook up for an abortion doctor?"

"Nothing like that," Mercy says. "Wait, you have a hook up for that?"

"I'm a modern woman living in a military state."

Mercy decides to spill the beans. "I need to get that sword out of the museum. The Temujin Death Sword."

Dee's eyes bug open. She puts a hand full over Mercy's mouth. "Are you crazy? There's ears everywhere."

"Sorry."

"We're going to have to go to my crib for this."

"You're inviting me to your home?"

"Don't get all excited. It's creepy."

They hop in a cab and drive uptown, way uptown, into the most shi-shi areas of the city. There are no cops anywhere, no black vans or Dogmen, no powerlines overhead. Just tastefully lit streets, private parks, and doormen wearing hats and bowties. Great Phillip Avenue is the kind of street where the Gold Star Insured get prescriptions delivered to their door by doctors living in the building.

"You sure you live here?" Mercy asks.

"Ms. Ellingsworth." The doorman bows as Dee walks in.

"Hanson," she replies, casually.

The doorman calls for the elevator, which is covered in red velvet.

"You're rich?" Mercy is shocked.

"Did I ever say different?"

"No, but—"

"My mom was the first Senior Vice President of cybersecurity at American Express. She came up with the algorithm that's kept credit card fraud to zero-point-one percent for the last nine years. That's how I got my start hacking. Learned a lot just sitting on her lap. And then when I got older, like a shit, I tried to break her code. Couldn't. But now she's all corporate management and fancy. I don't even think she codes anymore. Total sellout." The elevator reaches her floor and Dee is about to open the door when she turns to Mercy. "Listen, my mom thinks I'm gay and majoring in Women's Studies at VCU. So she's going to welcome you like you're marriage material. Do nothing to disabuse her of that. The only thing worse than her thinking we're having sex is her wondering if I'm going to date some Amex exec, get married and give her a grandkid, which is never happening. Clear?"

Mercy nods so they enter her apartment. It's posh AF. Expensive oil paintings on the wall, candelabras, and a grand piano. The most elegant woman Mercy had ever seen sits with a cup of tea and a newspaper by the fireplace.

"Dee, honey—that you?"

"Hi, mom. Just heading to my room," Dee says, quickly adding. "Oh, this is my friend, Mercy."

Dee's mom jumps up from her plush sofa chair like she's been goosed, and almost convulses with joy when she sees that her daughter has a brought home a 'friend.'

"Mercy, sweet Mercy, darling!" She strides towards them, arms wide open for a hug, and before Dee can say anything she envelops Mercy in her elegant silk-swathed body as if she's a long-lost relative. It's such a long hug that Mercy has to pull away. "Sorry," Dee's mother says. "I'm just overwhelmed—I mean happy—happy to meet a friend of Dee's. Finally. Where did you two meet? At VCU? A lesbian bar? You know I met Jonathan Richmond at a Trader Joe's once. Nice man. Are you too young to know his song 'I Was Dancing At A Lesbian Bar'? Probably…"

"Mom, stop!" Dee blushes.

"Oh, okay! But she's just lovely, isn't she? Just lovely! Mercy, consider yourself part of the family! What's mine is yours." She waves around the room as if Mercy is welcome to help herself to the priceless art on the wall.

"Mom."

"Dear?"

"You're kind of spoiling the mood, if you know what I mean?" Dee arches her eyebrow, and her mom snaps out of it, finally getting the picture.

"Of course! You do what you all do! Don't let me get in the way. So lovely to meet you, Mercy. Enjoy yourselves—that's what the body's for!"

"Mom!" Dee grabs Mercy's hand and leads her fast

down the hall. Mercy turns back and Dee's mom is waving and grinning.

"Your mom's a trip," Mercy says.

"After Dad split I think she wanted to be a lesbian—even designed a dating app for lesbians but never had the guts to use it herself. So she's fascinated that I may be Goldstar."

"Are you?"

"Fluid-sapio," Dee says. "Super square of you to ask."

Dee's room is like an Old School hip-hop museum. Framed Wu-Tang posters, Gang Starr and Mos Def albums, a wall of custom graffiti and a shrine honoring to MF DOOM replete with a cup filled with beer, a candle, and two voodoo dolls. Dee grabs a remote control from under her bed, and part of the graffitied wall flips to reveal the most futuristic coder set-up Mercy had ever seen. Several monitors lower from the bookshelves and start booting up and beeping. Dee takes a seat in front of the monitors and puts on a glowing headset and leather gloves like she's about to drive in Formula One. She types fast, and images and text spin across the screen until blueprints appear in 3D. Mercy doesn't recognize them right away.

"Our place of employ," Dee says. "The security system is in three zones. Each with its own separate security system that can never be turned off, even in an extended power outage. I'm actually impressed that these competing companies agreed to work together like this. Maybe some government initiative. Only weakness is that each system has to reboot for four minutes a day, but of course, that happens at different times, and they shift where security stands for those four minutes to get extra coverage. So there's really no way to get through any of this even if you were invisible, which you're not."

"So it's impossible?"

"Did I say that?" Dee shakes her head. "The key is communicating between the security company interfaces." Dee starts typing faster. Code fills the screen. Mercy paces around, useless, but after a few minutes can't take it anymore.

"What are you doing now?"

"Chatting with the security supervisor at Graystar asking for an exception, and then I'm going to get Hammer and Chesapeake Bay to do the same, so we'll have four minutes where all of the systems are coordinated to be down at once, but we won't be sure when that happens since they're not allowed to say."

"So how will we—"

"We won't. But I happen to know that these companies all have employee shifts that end at midnight, so if I had to guess, everyone I'm communicating with is off at midnight. They won't want a request like this to pass into the next shift since they'll have to explain it and probably oversee it after their shift is over since they got the request. So they're all going to probably do it at the same time, at least I think."

"And when does this have to happen?"

"Since it has to happen on the quarter-hour, per policy. We have exactly nineteen minutes." Dee sets her watch.

"What?"

"Let's go. Go!" Dee flips the table back and the computers disappear behind the graffiti wall. They sprint out of Dee's room and towards the elevator. "Bye Mom, we're heading back to the library to study for our Smash The Patriarchy final."

"Bye, Darlings! And come back soon, Mercy! You two feel so right together. Fit just like a velvet glove! Oh, there I go again… Text me, darlings—"

They get in the elevator and Mercy is about to call an

Uber when Dee reminds her that the less is traceable, the better. "Let's do lo-fi." Outside is a horse and carriage. Dee slips the man a hundred. "To the museum."

"On the double, Ms. Ellingsworth."

During the horse ride they go over the plan, but it changes as time gets slimmer. They arrive at the Museum with about a minute to spare. Dee just says, "Run as fast as you can."

"Nightshift," Dee tells the heavy-set security guard up front, who nods knowingly, more knowing that Dee hacked his phone and has texts proving that he has an expensive doily fetish that he's hiding from his wife. They run through Biodiversity until they reach the Exit near the bathrooms. Dee stops and checks her watch, which has the blueprints and a timer.

"Ten seconds—then, a straight line." She stares at her watch again. "Now!" They sprint down the hall and enter the stairway. "Okay, stop. Okay… now run!" They sprint the stairs until the third floor, where they land at the entrance to the Death Exhibit. Mercy is about to rush forward when a security guard walks right past them, swirling his keys. They crouch behind a kiosk and the guard looks both ways before holding his stomach and wincing. Then he walks off towards the bathrooms.

"Okay Mercy, we've got two minutes and change to get that sword out of there. And that starts right now." But Dee doesn't move forward. In fact, she walks to the wall and puts her hand on the fire alarm.

"Why aren't we going?" Mercy asks, panicked.

"You're going to tell me why we're doing this right now or I pull this alarm."

"Dee, now?"

"Why do you need this sword so bad?"

"Money," Mercy blurts out. "Lots of it. I know a collector who just wants to borrow it. And then I promise I'll put it back."

Dee rolls her eyes. "Screw it—I'm pulling the alarm."

"Okay!" Mercy says, desperate. "I dress up like a ninja and slice people's heads off for a company called Curated Ends. Then I use the money to pay for Health Insurance for my grandmother and her friend. I need the sword for a rich client who wants me to decapitate him with it. And that will give me the money I need to pay for Health Insurance without having to kill again, okay?"

Dee looks at her thoughtfully for a moment, considering all the gravity of what she's just heard confessed. Then she doubles over laughing. "You really had me there! Hahaha." But then she looks at Mercy again—her sweaty face full of guilt. "I knew it," Dee says.

"Will you help me?"

"For now." They head into the Death Exhibit and to the glass encasement where the Temujin Death Sword is held elegantly on a bamboo plank. Mercy is about to smash it when Dee pulls out a high-tech laser from her bag and begins slicing a grapefruit-sized hole through the glass like it's made of paper. She places a suction device on the glass and pulls off a perfect circle. It trips a local alarm, but Dee uses her phone to turn it off before it triggers the central alarm.

"You're goddamn Jane Bond," Mercy says.

Dee holds up her phone to show the timer. "Fifty-eight seconds."

Mercy reaches her hand through the hole and grips the famous ancient sword. Carefully, she slides it through the glass without touching the edges. She pulls the replacement sword out from her canvas bag. It's not even close to the original but the camera won't catch the difference if they're lucky. Mercy slides that into place and Dee reseals the glass when they hear a humming behind them. It's the security guard back from the bathroom.

"Hey!" the guard calls out. He grabs for his walkie.

Mercy grips the sword, take a step forward and goes full ninja gymnast. She flips in the air until she lands right in front of the stunned security guard and conks him on the head with the handle of the sword. He collapses to the floor, along with his walkie talkie.

Dee walks over and stares at Mercy, impressed. "You really are a killer."

"Let's go." They fly back down the stairs, dash through the Mammoth Pavilion, and they've just passed the last of the cameras when they see them: Chin, McGroarty and Kiki crouched behind a display of stuffed hyenas. The idiots look both ways and head up towards the Death Exhibit. Guess Fanny didn't trust Mercy to get the job done and sent them too. Dee gives Mercy the sign and they move on. They're just about to pass security when Mercy's cellphone starts buzzing in her pocket. It's Nick. When she goes to answer, Dee looks at her like she's insane.

"Hey," Mercy whispers. "In a movie. Can I call you back?—Nick, why are you crying?—I'll be right there."

Dee rolls her eyes as Mercy tucks her phone away. They run low, goose-step past the guard and out the door, Temujin Death Sword and all.

"You answered your phone?" Dee asks Mercy, shaking her head.

"Ethelfled's really sick," Mercy replies, like why even ask. She starts running down the street towards his apartment. "Thanks, Dee. You're the best! I'll explain everything later!"

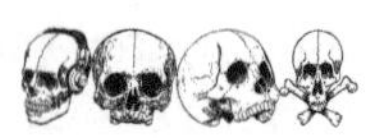

Nick opens his apartment door holding Ethelfled in his arms like a baby. Tears stream down his cheeks. "She's been vomiting and shaking," he says. "The vet said that if it happens again they'll recommend putting her down, and I can't, I just can't..." His voice is scratchy. Ethelfled whines a bit, but wags her tail seeing Mercy.

"No one's doing anything you don't want," Mercy says. "But if she's in pain, she should see a vet, okay?"

"Um, okay... But I don't want to do anything."

Mercy manages to get them downstairs and into an Uber. When they arrive at the vet, they're led to a cold bright room. A veterinarian enters with a knowing look.

"She's suffering," the vet tells Nick after examining the dog. "In this case we recommend pentobarbital by injection."

A nurse with latex gloves enters with a solemn face. Nick breaks down in tears. He buries his face into Ethelfled and sobs openly.

"We need a few minutes," Mercy says.

As soon as the vet leaves Nick breaks down. "She's been with me since the beginning. I found her as a puppy in an alley while I was in training. And I used to bring her back to the alley to visit. And she always seemed so proud when we got there like she wanted to show me where she came from. She would look through the trash and bring me a treat. Like an empty bag of Doritos. Once a rat. And then she'd look at me like it was time to go. And I can't let her go like this."

"Then let's get out of here," Mercy says. She walks Nick out with Ethelfled in his arms. The nurse stops Mercy in the hall, and looks both ways.

"What you do is your choice," the nurse says. "But this will be the most peaceful way." She hands Mercy a little cup with two yellow pills.

"Thanks." Mercy takes the cup.

"A half-blind three-legged dog named Ethelfled? I have a heart too."

Outside, they get into a waiting cab. "Eighth and Brunswick," Mercy tells the driver. "One last time, okay?"

They stand at the edge of a grimy alley on the Eastside of town. Nothing but garbage cans and rusted ladders hanging down from ramshackle apartment buildings. Nick places Ethelfled gently on the ground. Her three legs shake but she looks up at Nick with a fully human smile. Her tail wags and her whole body moves with the motion. Nick pulls out some kibbles and gives them to the dog. Mercy then hands him the paper cup. Nick kneels, takes the two yellow pills out and holds them in front of Ethelfled. The dog looks up at Nick with a proud smile and eats those two. Then, with an energy it hadn't had before, she scampers down the alley wagging her tail. Nick sniffles. The dog goes to the garbage, sniffs around. She finds something tasty. Then she returns to Nick. In Ethelfled's mouth is a flattened box of Trojans. Truly, the dog is human. Nick takes the package. He laughs out loud and then sobs and then laughs again. Mercy is not immune and wipe tears from her cheek. Ethelfled looks so proud like she's told the best joke ever, done the best set of stand-up. Nick picks the dog up and pets her on the forehead.

"Good girl. Always such a good girl."

Chapter 8

Beheading a wealthy eccentric with an eight-hundred-year-old Mongol Death Saber belonging to Genghis Khan appeals to my sister Mercy, she'll admit that much. But mainly it's the money. Four hundred grand is a windfall, not to mention a path to freedom for her, Nan and Maude. This gig must be making a truckload for Fanny too or she never would have agreed to Mercy's terms. Either way there's a spring in Mercy's step as she heads to the location. This is the kill that gets her out of killing for good, onto the straight and narrow towards stand-up comedy greatness.

Since the police infiltration, Curated Ends relocated to an unfinished office building on the south side of town. The building is eerie in that it appears to have almost been finished but then was abandoned altogether, as if the workers just picked up their tools and walked. Must have run out of money. Fanny worked out connecting the power undetected so there's reliable electricity, but there's no doors in certain places where they should be. Security turnstiles are set up in the lobby without gating. A freight elevator is in working order but there are no numbers on the buttons. Mercy presses the top button, and after a slow ride the doors open to what appears to be an unfinished office space. Electrical wires poke out of the wall where sockets might be, and slabs of wood are stacked neatly on the floor, perhaps where shelving was to be built. Windows are blacked out at the far end of the space, where an enormous curtain is set around a makeshift stage.

Onstage they've created a classic Dojo scene. A Japanese-inspired room with two bamboo mats, a low table with rice bowls, and two suits of armor staged on the wall and some calligraphy art. Carlos probably recreated a scene from Seven Samurai.

"Where's Gus?" Mercy asks Carlos when she sees him.

"Flu-like symptoms," he replies. "He said to wish you luck."

Fanny enters and is careful to show Mercy the Death Directive video right away.

"He's some tech genius. Made an app called Samurai Finance—he's obsessed with everything Samurai, hence the sword."

In the video, a handsome, square-jawed man in his early seventies describes a rare auto-immune disease that he is stuck with and the impossibility of survival despite every medical intervention money can buy. Then he gives his living will and instructions, "I don't want to die like a coward in the hospital. I must die in battle by the Temujin Death sword, like the Japanese Samurai did when they faced Genghis Khan and his Mongol horde." His special instructions include an agreement that he is to inspect the sword for authenticity before the kill.

Fanny told Mercy that it has already checked out. Thank God. Mercy doesn't feel like getting into it with Fanny, who almost certainly sent the three goons that night, but word at the museum is that there was a break-in and that three punks smashed up the Death exhibit and grabbed the sword, but not before murdering that security guard who Mercy had knocked unconscious.

Gus let Mercy know that McGrorty and Kiki came right to Fanny with the replacement sword Mercy had slid into the glass case, and even Fanny laughed at how fake it was compared to the photos. Gus took particular joy in describing the look on McGrorty's face when he walked out penniless with a worthless stick in his hands. "You could hear the sad trombone."

Fanny closes the video and Mercy accepts the terms. When it's time, she's told to set aside her usual masked ninja outfit and put on an elaborate armor worn by the Mongols of the time. Hardened leather and iron, laced together tightly with silk, and an iron war mask. Heavy, but not cumbersome, her body moves surprisingly well once she gets it all on. The client, Mercy is told, will have a wooden sword and chain-link armor but nothing around his neck, and so the fight is meant to be a minute tops—some light swordplay before the kill. There's even choreography instructions on his Death Directive tape. Mercy peels back the curtain and sees the man sitting cross-legged on the bamboo mat eating a bowl of rice with chopsticks. Like in a Bruce Lee film there's light tension music playing in the Japanese style, a nice touch by Carlos who is also probably making a bundle on this one as well.

"Mongol," the man says to Mercy when she steps onstage. He places his chopsticks down next to the rice bowl. "I have waited many years to face you. And to die by your sword. But I will not make it easy." He stands up with a wince. Seeing his face, Mercy recognizes him as that guy the magazines call Boy Wonder, a wink to the boundless energy of a man far older than most of the app developers he competes against. He's gone bald now, probably from his treatment, but his swath of lush orange hair was a trademark. This man could afford any doctor in the world to give him a safe death. He could be surrounded by his many admirers. But he wanted this. And now his legend will grow. Boy Wonder, CEO of Samurai Industries, dies by the sword of the great Genghis Khan, stolen from a museum. Money is expendable. This death will be legendary.

Boy Wonder puts a helmet on and unsheathes his wooden sword. Mercy bows and raises her sword to fight. Can the Boy Wonder fight? Surprisingly well. His swordplay is fluid and almost playful. There's joy in it but also precision. And Mercy does see that glimmer of fear in his eyes, and a hope that he might defeat her, millions of years of genetic programming telling him to survive above all else. But his eyes also reveal that he's sick and he accepts defeat as Mercy's sword pierces him. She finishes him in the way he requested. His suit of armor goes one way and his helmet another. For a reason Mercy can't explain, she doesn't freeze up after it is over, or imagine the death from his point of view. She doesn't see herself as a young girl or our father being killed, and Mom dragged away into a black van. It is just death. Could it be because she's free?

Carlos begins taking down the velvet curtain, eager to get this pop-up down quickly and pack up as soon as possible.

"Stellar job," Fanny says. She hands Mercy a manila envelope that is heavy and thick. Unlike all the times that Mercy simply shoved the money into her bag, this time she counts it and holds it to her chest. Freedom. Nan and Maude's freedom from fear of the unknown and the danger of the Wellspring.

"So, I guess this is it?" Fanny asks. To Mercy's surprise, Fanny tears up. "I know I've been a hard-ass. But you've always been my favorite. Good luck to you, Mercy. Go make 'em laugh."

"Thanks for everything, Fanny," Mercy says before

walking off. She zips the envelope of money into her canvas bag along with the Temujin Death Sword, which Dee and her plan to return to the museum in a way that will cause mystery and suspicion (and probably an updated security system). But now it's time for Mercy to get out of there. Put all this death behind her and move forward with her life. She steps onto the freight elevator and presses the button down. She's surprised to be a bit emotional, like she's leaving behind a chapter of her life that taught her many lessons. But she's also thinking about a future of lying in bed with Nick, watching old movies and eating Flamin' Hot Cheetos without a worry in the world, when the lights flicker on and off and the elevator stops mid-floor.

"Perfect," Mercy says out loud.

She clicks the buttons, but nothing works. Some kind of power outage. She pokes at the ceiling, and it gives with the force of the sword. She's able to move aside the slat and is just about to climb up when the elevator suddenly jolts back to life. It continues down and Mercy shrugs. But it travels past the lobby floor and keeps going several stops below. Then the door opens to some kind of basement storage space. It's dark and cold down there, with flickering lights in the distance. Mercy sees tall cages, probably set up for tech that never made it in. She pushes the elevator buttons again but they're really dead this time. She peeks out into the low light. There's got to be an emergency stairwell somewhere.

"Hello?" Mercy asks, "Anyone here?"

She steps out of the elevator and finds herself at the end of a long hallway. It smells like sawdust and paint fumes. She hears the vague sound of metal clanging rhythmically against a wall. The sound echoes down the hallway like a wrench being tapped against pavement. Mercy reaches for the sword and steps towards the sound, her heart speeding up. Halfway down the hallway, there's a standing electric fan set in front of an empty beer can on its side. The force of the air from the fan pushes the can forward until it hits the wall with a clank, then it rolls slowly back when the fan turns, until it is pushed to the wall again. Every time the can almost reaches the fan, the fan turns, and the can is forced back to the wall. There's a metaphor there, something Greek, but Mercy wonders what kind of sociopath set that up before abandoning ship for another construction site. Mercy breathes a sigh of relief and turns back to look for the exit and that's when an enormous figure descends from above and hits her with some kind of steel pipe. Her instincts make her shift at the last millisecond, so she takes some of the force away, but her shoulder blade cracks and the strength of the hit winds her enough that the attacker is able to run off down the hall into the darkness. Mercy drops her canvas bag and steadies her sword with her left arm, her right arm having gone numb. She looks up and sees that there's a ledge where he must have been waiting for her. Maybe this is his home, and he just wants her out.

"I'm leaving, okay?" Mercy shouts into the darkness. "I won't tell anyone you're squatting. Honestly, I don't care."

But she's barely done saying that before another attacker runs up from behind her and slams her in the neck. She steadies her sword and rolls beneath the next strike—she swerves and lunges at whoever the fuck this next crazy asshole is, and she feels a clean flesh cut sting the back of her neck. The second assailant stands in the distance, shielded by darkness. Soon the big one is back, and they both stand glaring at her as she holds out the deadly sword towards them.

"I'm going to count to three, and after that I won't be so nice," Mercy says, ready to kill whatever or whoever the fuck speaks. But they are silent. Mercy's eyes turn cat-like and she makes out their frames— one big and thick, the other short and squat with big hair. She looks up at the ledge again and standing there casually is the third, with his stupid mohawk and acne scars. "Oh Christ, you three idiots?" Mercy ask. "Lemme guess, you couldn't get the samurai gig and now you want the money? Well then let's fucking play. Fanny's going to have your nuts anyway."

McGrorty chuckles. "She still doesn't get it."

"What's to get, genius?"

"Can't have you out there retired, telling stories with no skin in the game," he replies. "Fanny told us to take what's ours. The sword, the money, and your scalp. Now that was an offer we couldn't refuse."

"Bullshit," Mercy says, but it all rings true. Fucking Fanny. After she's done with these three, Mercy will impale her too. Guess her killing isn't done after all.

"Let's make a deal," Mercy says, trying to buy time as her eyes adjust more fully. "I take the money and the sword and the three of you go fuck yourselves."

It's the last hilarious thing that my sister is able to say before a flash of light illuminates Chin and Kiki, and Mercy realizes that she's been shot. Her mouth juts open with a spurt of hot blood. She buckles to the ground and rolls forward, aware that the gun is still above her, looking for another shot. But she moves in slow motion, rolling, pathetically, right to Chin and Kiki's feet. She lifts her sword to cut their legs off but it's like lifting a slab of marble. Her lungs become a weighted blanket. Chin grins down at her, and Mercy hears McGrorty snort. He jumps down from the ledge and waves his gun around. Mercy tries again to swing her sword, but misses, and Kiki jumps and kicks her face. The force of the kick shifts the mechanics of Mercy's jaw—unhinges it from her face, and blood gushes in a pool beneath her cheek. She tries focusing on breathing and not drowning in her own blood when another boot connects with her ribs, probably from that asshole with the mohawk. He raises his boot and pushes down on her face. Mercy's vision blurs from the searing pain. She grabs the foot and manages to spin him off. Then she goes for her sword again with her good hand but a boot lands on her wrist, crushing it under the weight. Bones crack.

"Bitch almost sprained my ankle," McGroarty complains.

"Guess it's not your day, Ninja Girl." McGrorty looks down at Mercy, pityingly. He picks up her canvas bag and opens the manila envelope. The money. Her freedom. Nan and Maude's safety. Mercy wills herself to move again, but her arms are definitely broken. She can barely raise them. A sick laugh emanates from Kiki.

"Can I finish her?"

"Let's ask her," McGrorty says. "Hey, Ninja Girl. I'm going to give you a final choice. Either Kiki here shoots you in the head like a dog, or we hand you back the sword and let you commit ritual suicide. Apparently, women Samurai do it by slitting their throats. What'd you say it was called?"

"Jigai," Mercy coughs out.

"Right, Jigai. So what do you say, Ninja Girl? It's your death." Mercy gives McGrorty a nod, and he understands what she wants. "Help her up," he directs Chin.

"There's no time for games," Kiki says.

"I said, help her up! I want to watch it. Plus, if we ever get caught for this, they can call it a suicide."

Chin pulls Mercy's limp body off the floor. There are bones broken in places she can't even imagine, not to mention a hot bullet stuck inside her. Still, they get Mercy to her knees. And they put the sword in her hand, and angle it to her neck. Mercy takes hold of the handle.

"Bye, Bye, Ninja."

The blade is cold and sharp at her neck and Mercy can feel the sting as she pushes it into her skin. She takes one last breath, gathering the strength for a clean cut— a final swift kill. But as she's about to thrust the blade into her own jugular there's another blast of light and Mercy probably thinks: "Bastards shot me anyway." Maybe she tries to feel the bullet enter because she wants to know what finally takes her out. Maybe she wonders if this is what our dad felt? Or what I might have felt in my death? But there's nothing in her head other than more flashes of light and the excruciating pain and the sound of screaming and struggling.

The sword at her neck lowers and her body falls to the ground like a rag doll— all of her limbs are numb— and her face smashes against the concrete floor in a puddle of warm blood. She keeps her eyes open for as long as she can. She sees bodies flailing and a spray of blood wets her cheek. Chin, the big man, falls in front of her— stunned eyes wide open like the decapitated heads she's left at Curated. More gunshots and yelling.

"Let's get the fuck out of here, Jimmy!" Kiki yells.

Mercy hears other voices too. Familiar ones.

"Do you know me?" Mercy asks, but the words gurgle weakly in her mouth. "Do you know me?..."

Chapter 9

My sister Mercy is nine years old at yet another drab government office. She doodles in a My Little Pony coloring book that's been torn and mostly filled in by other recent orphans like her. Across from Mercy is a pale man in an ugly brown tie who looks like he hasn't had a decent night's sleep in years. A big stack of folders are piled on his desk and Mercy knows intuitively that she represents one of those folders, and that he's dying to get through whatever problem she represents fast. He gives her a weary look and sighs. Mercy's in pom-poms, the same ice cream-stained clothes she wore when our parents were taken and her world exploded into a million pieces.

"You got any brothers or sisters?"

"Theo. He's at boarding school. I miss him."

"I see."

Mercy looks back down at the coloring book and tries to color a rainbow, but all the fun colors are gone so she's filling the sky in brown. She does her best to make clean edges, like a good little girl, which she still is at this point. The phone on the man's desk rings and he picks it with a grunt.

"Well, bring them in already," he says.

Mercy's filling in the sun with a maroon color when the door opens.

"Mercy, dear sweet girl." It's Nan. She's younger, skin just starting to break, and suggestions of gray spreading lightly at the roots. Maude and Ester are there too—so much more youthful too, full of color and life.

"You're the girl's grandmother?" the man asks Nan.

"I am."

"And we're her support system," Maude butts in, presenting Ester too.

Mercy likes the sound of that and cracks a smile. Like there's a system specially built to support each person. But Mercy looks up at the faces of her support system, Nan, Maude, and Ester—she sees through their smiles a deep, horrified concern, and it occurs to Mercy that only someone who's in deep trouble needs a support system. So she start to cry, her first cry since she's been alone.

"Dad's dead." She sobs. "But Mom… when's she coming back?"

They all look to the man for an answer. He purses his lips and shakes his head.

"Honey." Nan places a hand on her shoulder. "Your mother is getting the medical treatment she needs at a new facility. The best treatment money can buy. At a place called the, uh… Wellspring, they're now calling it. Where she can get well."

Maude winces.

Nan crouches down to Mercy's eyelevel. "You know that momma's been sick? Well, after that terrible Vogovin Virus hit, a lot of people got scared."

"I thought they found a cure?"

"They did, honey. But there's still a lot of fear when someone falls ill. So there's a treatment center not too far away. Momma's going to get the medical care she needs to get, and she'll come back healthy."

"What about Theo? Can he come home now?"

"I'm afraid that's not possible with the state lockdown. He wants to come home, but he can't. So for now, you're going to come with us, and we're going to have a sleepover and we're all going to watch movies and eat ice cream just like we did Easter weekend. Would you like that?"

"Yes," Mercy says. "But Nan?"

"Yes, dear?"

"I don't think I want to have ice cream anymore."

The man looks at the four of them wearily and hands Nan a file. "It's all in there, everything you need," he says. "Good luck."

Nan grabs the folder and leads Mercy out of the office by hand, into her car, and off to Cedarville Apartments. There, Mercy is a project and a puzzle. They gather around her—a cereal-eating, pom-pom-wearing, cartoon-watching question mark in ill-fitting clothes. Maude, Ester, and Nan watch Mercy curiously, attentively, lovingly, wondering how in hell this little girl dropped in their lap and how she will survive?

"What happened to you should never happen to a little girl," Nan explains to Mercy on the first night. "And I wish I can tell you that your parents and your brother are coming back soon." Nan sees Mercy get hopeful, raising her eyes. "But they're not. Your mom and dad are never coming back, dear. Your brother either, at least not for a long while. The sooner you're told that the better off you are. We're your new family. Me, Maude, and Ester. And we're going to protect you. And keep you safe. But we're also going to make sure you know how to take protect yourself. So that you never have to feel scared, okay?"

Mercy nods, but has no idea what she's talking about.

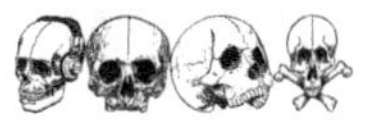

That was the last sit-down for a while. Soon after, my death certificate arrives so Mercy loses hope of ever seeing me again either. That's when phase two begins. The three old ladies, Mercy's Guardians, take her to a training facility in an abandoned part of town next to an auto mechanic shop. It's owned by a thick, bald man with a Russian accent. Mercy watches Nan go into his office and talk for a while. They both gesticulate with their hands and Nan slaps his desk. The man leans back in his chair, throws his hands in the air as if there's nothing to do. Nan pleads, then seems to threaten him, and the man looks out at Mercy through the window. She sees pity in the man's eyes and it's too much to bear since she thinks she's going to cry again, so she looks away. The man stands up, an irritated expression on his face as he walks up towards Mercy. He's enormous, a Russian giant with huge, hairy wrists and an ample stomach that looks impenetrable—his steps seem to dent the floor.

"You frightened of me?" he ask Mercy, reading her mind.

"I'm done being frightened," Mercy says. Her response makes him grunt like she passed a test he didn't want her to pass. "What's your name anyway?"

"No name until you earn name," the Russian Bear says.

"Okay."

"Ever carry sword?" he asks. She shakes her head. He pulls a wooden stick off a rack and holds it out with his big meaty fist—his forearm pulsing like Popeye. "Take this from me," he says. Mercy looks at him, wide-eyed. Then he yells, "I said, take it!"

The last time Mercy heard anyone yell at anyone was once when Dad yelled at Mom about money and she pulled back and kicked him right in the center, up through his legs, so hard she saw his eyes pop out of his head. He stopped yelling after that and actually started laughing eventually.

Mercy goes to grab the wooden sword, but instead of trying to take it she uses it as a bar to add power as she leaps forward and unleashes all of her weight into a kick that lands square between his legs. The Russian Bear lets out a horrible roar. His face and his entire body turn red, and he pulls back like he's going to hit her, but instead he throws the wooden sword to the ground. Mercy watches him take in the pain with deep breaths in a crouched position, screaming Russian words that she would only later understand. Mercy steps forward and picks the wooden sword off the ground.

"Do I get to know your name yet?"

The man looks up at Mercy like she's insane. Mercy sees that Nan, Maude, and Ester snicker. The man looks at them like they've just burned down his village. Then he gathers himself. He looks off into the distance and says, "We start tomorrow." Then he stomps away and slams his office door.

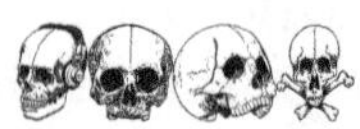

Mercy is nine years old and The Russian Man is slapping away her feeble attempts at stabbing him with a wooden sword, calling her a lazy shit. She's ten and he's yelling over her as she repeats a painful backflip into a stab over and over. She's eleven and twelve and thirteen and doing knuckle push-ups and leaping over buckets and planking while he hits her with sticks and berates her with Russian words that would make a marine blush. Fourteen, fifteen, sixteen, seventeen and it's hit-hit—punch-punch-kick, over and over—until her knuckles are raw and bleeding. She jumps over sticks and summersault into the splits, and he smashes her over and over again and she guard-guard-push-and-slides to create an inch of room to push forward with her stick. She reaches through the space and her stick finds room and she strikes him hard across the neck and he looks even more stunned than she does, like the time she first kicked him in the balls so many years before. The Russian Bear appears ready to maul her, but he takes his coiled energy and stops. Then he bows.

"Well done," he says. His body goes slack like he's finally able to relax after all these years. Mercy can see how the time he's put in has affected him, with deep wrinkles and graying at his temples. "Today you graduate." He pulls out an enormous cigar and lights it right then and there. He takes several big puffs, let's out a massive jet of smoke, and then hands it to Mercy. She doesn't know what to do with it but has seen enough movies that she takes a drag and starts to cough fire from her throat. He chuckles.

"I am Vladislav," he says and offers his hand to shake. "Friends call me Vlad."

Mercy coughs more, this time out of shock. "I'm your friend?"

"I don't know," he says.

"Thank you for everything… Vlad," Mercy says and bows.

He bows again too. Then he looks her up and down, takes back his cigar, and walks away. Mercy watches him enter his office and close his door. He looks at Mercy one last time through the glass, and she recognizes a slight quiver in his lower lip that she once saw when he talked about his village in Russia and his family who never made it out.

Nan, Maude, and Ester wait outside, like always. They're older too. Maude has a cane with a cool eagle head on the top. Ester is looking a little less sharp than before, even bewildered.

"Let's celebrate," Nan says.

And they all laugh, and Ester laughs, but blood comes out of her mouth, and she looks down at her stomach and there's a sword poking through.

"You did this to me," Ester points. "Murderer!"

Mercy turns to Nan and Maude, hoping they don't know what she's saying but they've transformed into McGroarty and Kiki. "Where's my fucking money?" They scream and a gun goes off. Mercy's head bursts like a grape and her body falls into a dark void and she can't move her limbs, and her killers gaze down at her ghoulishly and morph into a bright light that yanks her body from the abyss, and she tastes vinegar and dirt and hears horrible screeches, and she lurches to consciousness and some woman in a surgical mask peers down at her. On the fringes of her vision Mercy sees Dee, Nan, Maude, Gus, and also Vladislav, or Vlad as his friends called him, all seated around her. And then her eyes go cross, and she fades out once again.

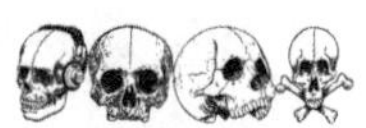

When Mercy comes to they're all there but this time it's dark, save for the dim florescent lights around her hospital bed. Everyone is asleep on chairs, drooling and snoring: Nan, Maude, Dee, Gus, and the Russian Bear Vladislav. He actually looks normal-sized next to Gus. Mercy is aware of where she is and that against all the odds, she's alive. There are wires and tubes around her and stuck in her. A tube is in her nostrils helping her breathe and another tube feeding her. She calms herself, trying to get used to the dull pain around her jaw and her ribs, and for some reason her ankle is killing. She knows she's alive or at least half alive, and that the people in this room are likely responsible for that. Her mouth is so dry that her tongue feels like sandpaper and she's craving ginger ale for some reason, but when she tries to call for a nurse nothing comes out, maybe a hoarse honk. Gus, in his tiny chair tries to re-arrange himself but wakes up momentarily to see that Mercy is staring at him. He jolts up and that wakes Dee, and the others start to wake too, like creaky dominoes.

"Don't try to move," Gus says.

Mercy attempts to speak again but nothing comes out. Still, that makes Gus smile. Dee's up and shaking her head like Mercy did something stupid again and this time she has proof. Maude looks miserable as she is woken by Dee, and so does Vlad. Finally, Maude nudges Nan.

"Wake up, Nanette. Our girl lives."

Nan opens her eyes and sits up. She walks to Mercy's bedside and lays a gentle hand on her arm. "Nod if you understand me, Mercy," she says. Mercy nods slightly and pain shoots up her neck. "Good. Because you have got some serious explaining ahead of you."

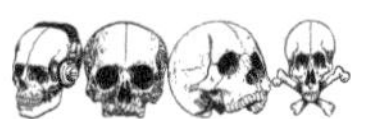

Mercy is on her third jar of applesauce. Her appetite is finally making itself heard above the painkillers. She's had a War Room around her for weeks. They pace and throw their arms in the air. They interrogate her, and Mercy tells them everything, mainly with nods and whispers of confirmation. Even about Ester. Nan and Maude have to leave the room for a while to take that in and who can blame them? Mercy cries the whole time they're gone, and they don't let her off the hook easy. When they're done berating her for her carelessness and selfishness and stupidity, Maude sums it all up like she's Perry Mason, "So all this time we thought you were focusing on comedy you've been sneaking into a curated death business to work as a ninja assassin, and all so you could pay health insurance for me, Ester and your grandmother? And then when you finally get the gig that's going to bring you the motherload and keep up safe from the Wellspring you get your ass trounced by some jealous competitors?"

"We need to get those motherfuckers," Gus and Dee say at the same time, and it occurs to Mercy that bringing together Gus and Dee was some kind of genetic imperative.

"To kill them will not be a problem," Vlad speaks. "But it is the government system that is real problem. We must take down whole system."

"Spoken like a true commie," Dee says. They must have become acquainted too because Vlad grins when she says that instead of smashing her.

"The Wellspring?" Gus says. "No one even knows where it is."

"Four crazy broads, King Kong Bundy, and Vlad the Impaler? We'll find it." Maude says.

And they're all laughing now—hooting even—when the door creaks open, and it's a damn good thing they stopped plotting a government takeover because it's a cop. Well, it's Mercy's cop. Nick F. Black enters holding flowers still wrapped from Trader Joe's. He steps in the door sheepishly, and Mercy gets why, because everyone gives him a furious glare until they see Mercy smile and they make the connection.

"Oh, so this is the famous Nick F. Black?" Dee asks, looking him up and down. "You took my girl's virginity. Grocery store orchids is the best you could do?"

"She said she likes orchids, so I thought—"

"Want I should beat him to pulp?" Vlad asks, and Nick shudders at Vlad's sheer size.

"I'll help," Gus says.

"No need for help," Vlad says, and they squabble about who gets to crush Nick, right in front of him.

Eventually Dee steps. "If you beat him up we'll have to worry about his hospital bills and that will be expensive," she says. "Better to just kill him."

"So we kill," Vlad says to Gus, and they take a step forward.

"Now, now, enough," Nan says, and everyone loosens up and smiles like it was always a joke, but neither Nick nor Mercy are entirely convinced. Nan turns to Nick. "It's nice to meet you, Nick." And then she hugs him, squashing the flowers on his chest. "Oh, muscles!" she says, but then whispers in his ear, "hurt her and I'll hunt you," because his face goes white again. Through all this Mercy reaches for her makeup and tries to at least apply some base. Her jaw's been relocated but it's puffy and red. She probably looks like a mutant.

"We're all going to get a snack," Nan says to the group. When Dee ignores her Nan is like, "You too, Dee."

Dee reluctantly leaves the room, and each of Mercy's protectors look Nick and up and down, measuring him like he's prey who got lucky for now.

"They seem nice," Nick says once the room empties. Then, awkwardly, he holds out his squashed orchids.

"Put them with the rest of it." Mercy gestures towards a side table that is bare but for a box of Kleenex.

"I called you over and over," Nick says. "I thought you ghosted me. I nearly crashed when your friend texted me that you were in the hospital. A random attack... Do you have any idea who did this?"

"Cops were already here to interrogate me," Mercy says, acting a little irritated to throw him off his questioning. "You can read the report."

"Sorry... I'm sorry," he says. "When someone you care about gets you hurt—"

"Just sit with me, 'kay?"

Nick looks defeated as he sits by her side. He kisses her hand. And then, like a little bitch, he starts to cry. "Sorry," he says, wiping away tears. "I just..."

"Do something for me?"

"Anything."

"There's an US Weekly on the chair. The one with Blue Ivy on the cover. Read it to me?"

Nick grabs the magazine, and like a good boyfriend he sits bedside and reads Mercy the trash mag, pausing to show her pictures of celebrities walking out of rehab, weight loss gone wrong, and Billie Eilish's insane Academy Award speech, like a parent with a Dr. Seuss book. Mercy can finally relax.

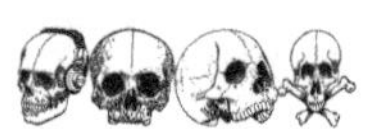

Five more shitty weeks in the hospital recovering. The cops visit multiple times. They try to connect the dead body found in the basement of Fountain Tower with what happened to Mercy, but nothing sticks. Mercy was always good at keeping secrets. They even bring up the Temujin Death Sword which went missing from the very museum where Mercy works, but Dee proves her genius because there's no trace of them on the security footage, only McGroarty, Kiki, and Chin. Dee even scrubbed out the times when that gang visited the Death exhibit on their clock. She's an Alpha hacker, and Mercy owes her a thousand times over.

Finally, Mercy checks out of the hospital on a rainy Tuesday. Uninsured, the hospital bill would have cost several mansions and she'd be long gone to the Wellspring, but she's safe for now. Mercy refuses to be wheeled out, so she limps as Nan leads her to an Uber and manages to get her in. Nan's been feeding her beet soups in the hospital like it's her job and the nurses are dumbfounded at her quicker-than-usual recovery. They refer to Mercy as Wolverine. And Wolverine power is precisely what Mercy needs when she gets to Cedarville Apartments and has to walk the nine flights of stairs. But when she does finally reach the top, and Nan unbolts the locks she feels even more like a superhero because her Marvel Universe is waiting inside. Dee has set up an elaborate computer system in the kitchen, and Maude, Dee, Vlad, Gus, and also Nick crowd around looking at security cam footage.

"Bingo," Dee says, pointing to the screen. "The killers have emerged."

No one had been able to find McGroarty and Kiki since the day they shot Mercy and stole her money and the sword. And yet there they are in black and white, playing cards in a luxury hotel casino.

"Gabiglia Hotel," Dee says. "They're in the ten K a night penthouse spending your money like it's doomsday. Hookers, Louis V bags, drugs. You're lucky McGroarty also knows how to count cards because he's been making most of it back at the blackjack table."

"They won't even notice when we sneak in and kill them," Vlad says.

"I'm going to leave now," Nick says, covering his ears. He hugs Mercy sweetly. "Call me after. And please, be careful."

They kiss, and everyone turns away, but Vlad growls, so Nick heads for the door. That's when Maude walks in with her knitting bag. She pulls out a wrapped gift and lays it on the table. "I don't just do scarves," she says. "You're a superhero, after all— you need a look." Mercy unwraps the paper and it's a full-body Ninja outfit with red thunderbolts on the Luchador-inspired mask. It's amazing. Mercy starts to cry as she hugs her. "Made entirely of Litton—this crazy iron synthetic that's light like cotton but can stops bullets. I mean, it would hurt like hell, but…"

"It's amazing," Mercy says. She looks at Nan and her three wonderful friends Gus, Dee, and Vlad. "Let's go hunt down some bad guys?"

"But first," Nan says. "How about a bath? You smell like a skunk's tomb."

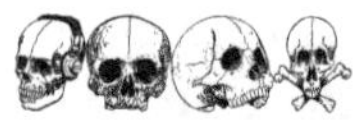

Two weeks later, at 11:54 p.m., they enter the lobby of the Gabiglia Hotel like they're Ocean's Fourteen. Nan and Maude are dressed like old ladies, which they kind of are, but it's never been so pronounced—cardigans and reading glasses and drooping pantyhose puts on years. Maude balances herself on a walker, which teeters precariously, like even the slightest wrong move will send her careening to the floor. Nan wears a bonnet and horn-rimmed glasses and carries her purse out in front of her like a kid on Halloween. Dee struts in wearing gaming headphones and an Adidas tracksuit. She sits down on a lobby couch and immediately opens her laptop, ready to work. Gus enters in a glittering wrestler's outfit with a cape made of the Russian Flag. He looks like he just came from a headline fight at the MGM Grand Stadium. Next to him in an all-black suit is Vlad, clearly the famous wrestler's Russian bodyguard. Mercy trails close behind in flip-flop sandals, a beach bag, and a towel thrown over her shoulders. Wearing flip-flops makes her limp less pronounced, like she's just straining to keep her footwear on. Thanks to Dee, they're all fixed for audio with tiny microphones that fit like dots inside their ears. The mics look like little moles, and there's even a slight hair poking out of Mercy's in case she gets apprehended.

"Flaming-Six-Tango—let's do this," Maude says as they enter, and her voice is appropriately shaky-grandma. And right then Team Crazy splits into different directions. Maude ambles to the center of the lobby and pulls a bolt from her walker—it comes apart as if it was held together by thread and the metal pieces splay in every direction as Maude falls flat on her face. Even on the thick-padded carpet the fall looks terrible. Maude immediately starts to moan. Nan looks down at her in shock, her purse still held out for effect, and screams at the top of her lungs.

"My wife has fallen, and she can't get up!"

Gus, in his outrageous wrestler's outfit, walks over and exclaims in his loud faux-Russian I accent. "I vill save her!"

But Nan sneers at Gus, "Not you, Nicolai Hammer. You're a bad man!"

She steps forward and slaps him in the face with her bag. It's such a bizarre scene that not only security but all of the attendants leave their posts to watch.

"You can't fool me, Old Lady Hutchinson!" Gus/ Nicolai Hammer says. "Vee know of your evil plan for vorld domination!"

"Help me!" Maude howls from the ground. "Someone help!"

It's high camp, drawing a crowd that wants to know if this is real or a Casino interactive theater experience. Nan steps to Gus and thwacks him with a foot to the balls. He crumbles to his knees and is now moaning several feet from Maude.

"Why won't someone help me?!" Maude yells to anyone who will listen.

Then Nan falls to the ground too and soon everyone is trying to help everyone. From her position on the couch, Dee gives Mercy a nod, and Vlad and her walk off to the elevators. The fourth one opens, as planned.

"Turning off cameras in five seconds. After that you'll have five minutes max," Dee says in their ears.

Once the elevator doors close, Mercy dips into her pool bag and grabs a black mask for Vlad. She slips on the crazy black and red Litton superhero outfit that Maude knit for her.

"Remember what I taught you," Vlad says.

"You taught me everything," Mercy replies.

When the elevator doors open, they walk low to the penthouse door ready to try one of the dozens of hacked room keys Dee provided, but the door is already ajar with a bottle of vodka stuck at the base. "Shame," Dee says to them. "I spent days working those out and these idiots leave the door open."

What they see inside is out of a gangster rap video or the movie Scarface. The penthouse is palatial in the Greek style, with marble pillars and water features and a circular bed on a raised platform that looks out over the city. McGroarty is asleep on the floor next to the bed with a bottle of mezcal between his legs. It's as if he almost made it to bed but not quite. The canvas bag, which Mercy sees has both money and the sword poking out of it is just sitting there right under his elbow. He's using a priceless ancient artifact of war and hundreds of thousands of dollars as a sort of drunk arm pillow. Vlad walks up to McGroarty and looks down at him almost pityingly but then leans over and stabs him in the neck with a small curved knife. McGroarty's eyes pop open and he looks shocked and desperate like he was resuscitated from a coma. He quickly grabs for his neck and dark blood runs down his fingers. Vlad grabs the canvas bag as McGroarty falls to the ground unable to speak or do anything to save himself. Vlad slides the bag across the room so that no blood will spray on it.

What McGroarty likely sees from his position of death is a massive masked man, but Mercy has this compulsion that it's too good a death for him. She steps forward and starts to peel back her mask. She wants him to see that it's the Ninja Girl back from the dead who did this to him. But as she lifts her mask Vlad stops her.

"He knows," Vlad says. And indeed, McGroarty has turned Mercy's way, and as blood spills down his chest and onto the marbled floor he looks even more shocked—the shock of knowing that after all they'd done to her, they hadn't finished the job. And then his neck turns to the side and it's as if all of the blood drained out of his body because he turns a sickly off-white only seen in fish markets. Mercy zips the canvas bag and throws it across her shoulder. Mission accomplished and time to go. But that's when they hear something from the other side of the penthouse. An off-tune rendition of Adele's "Hello." Vlad gives Mercy a nod and they head towards the sound.

The bathroom is Calcutta marble and arched ceilings—opulent in the way you would imagine Caesar's private bathhouse. The bathtub is huge and filled with so many bubbles that they almost can't see the back of Kiki's head poking out where she sings horribly. Vlad steps forward silently and Mercy follows but immediately steps on a discarded champagne bottle, which spins and hits the marble with a loud clank.

"McFluffer, is that you?" Kiki asks, bubbles all in her face. "Hand me a towel?"

When she sticks her arm out Mercy shrugs and pulls a towel off the rack. It's thick and soft and luxurious. Mercy hands it to Kiki and watches her pat bubbles off her face. It's so odd to see her without all the eyeliner. She looks childlike in a way. And Mercy is so transfixed that she doesn't even realize what she's opened her eyes to.

"Take whatever you want!" Kiki says and moves back along the tub. "Just don't kill me."

"But you killed me," Mercy can't help but reply. "It's only fair."

Then it must dawn on her who it is, and like her boyfriend in the other room, Kiki's skin goes fish-market white. "Truce?" she says, then she whips bath water and bubbles towards Mercy. She's fast enough to fall back and grab a handgun from behind the shampoo bottles. Mercy feels the wind of the bullet graze her neck before it embeds in the wall. Vlad pushes Mercy to the ground, steps forward, and knocks the gun out of the woman's hand. Kiki falls back into the tub and shrugs like you can't blame a girl for trying. Vlad grabs an electric hair dryer and drops it into the tub. There's a flash and Kiki convulses, and a gross smell emanates from the water as Mercy's final living murderer twitches off to death. Mercy lies on the ground in a pile of bubbles on the marble floor. She knows she screwed up bad and is going to hear it from Vlad.

"Hate to interrupt your spa time," Dee says in their ears. "But if you're not out of there in twenty seconds, you're going to be on the nightly news."

They rush out of the penthouse and get into the elevator. Vlad takes off his mask, and Mercy gets back into her pool wear and tucks away her ninja costume. Vlad notices blood on Mercy's neck. He pulls out the handkerchief from his suit and wipes it off.

Vlad frowns. "A hundred knuckle push-ups."

"I just got out of the hospital," Mercy say.

"Two hundred knuckle push-ups for complaining."

The elevator doors open, and they walk separate ways like it was just timing that put them in the same place at the same time. In the lobby, Team Crazy forms like Voltron. Dee already has her computer packed up and is heading towards the exit. Nan yells, "You come back here you villainous commie scumbag!" And she chases Gus out of the hotel, bag in the air, where he jumps into a waiting taxicab.

Maude turns to the entire lobby and says, "Each one of you will hear from my lawyers!" And with the pieces of metal that constituted her walker gathered in her arms, she struts out of the lobby like she's many years younger and not at all hampered by a walking impediment.

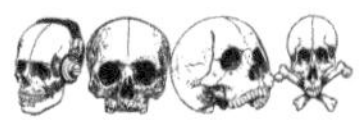

It's a forty-five-minute cab ride, but they all end up in front of Cedarville Apartments at the same time. They walk towards the stairs when Maude says, "Well, I'll be. They finally fixed the elevator." The Marvel Universe squeezes in.

"You could have taken it easy on the groin shot," Gus complains.

"It needed to be authentic," Nan replies, and they all laugh.

Inside the apartment they count the money in stacks. McGroarty and Kiki actually didn't do as much damage as they thought. After McGroarty lost thirty-grand on craps, the hotel started comping the room. And that's when he must have gone on a run because they only counted about thirteen grand gone in total. Three-hundred and eighty-seven thousand dollars left over.

"Enough to insure all of us for a while," Mercy says.

"Save it," Dee says, "I'm still on my mother's insurance. She put it in her new contract with Amex."

"I'm never sick," Vlad and Gus say simultaneously. "Take care of Maude and Nan. And yourself."

"Thank you." Mercy bows. She heads to the kitchen to help Nan with an apple pie. Mercy loves the overall laughter and frolicking going on. It's a real party. I must admit some FOMO here. What I wouldn't do to be part of my little sister's Marvel Universe party, celebrating a successful mission with apple pie. And Mercy is happier than she's been in forever. She's doing the actual cha-cha around the kitchen when a DM comes in from Nick.

Nick: You alive?

Mercy: *Yeah, but tired—you're going to have to be on top tonight (Eggplant emoji*). Yuck!

Nan puts the pie in the oven. Mercy dances out of the kitchen, ready for more fun, but there's silence in the den.

"Who died out here?" she asks, wondering why everyone is crowded around Dee's computer. They all turn to her, faces pale and severe. Dee gives Mercy a pitying look, and to her shock she sees that Maude is crying. Maude never cries. "What the hell's going on?"

"There's been a leak at The Wellspring."

There've been leaks before. Satellites photos of industrial buildings that look very much like hospitals. One photo got close enough to show some Sick people. And they looked, well, like Sick people out taking a walk. The Plastic President, Phyllis McCabe, was able to explain it away as part of their daily health routine. So Mercy wonders why the big hush. And then she looks at the screen. It's a black and white surveillance video that is about ten seconds long, and it takes her eyes a few seconds to unscramble it, but what she sees is a woman taking out what looks like garbage to a dumpster. The woman is thin and middle-aged but pretty and has her hair in two distinct puffs, giving her a silhouette like Minnie Mouse. The woman looks up at the sky, stretching like she hasn't seen the outside in months and wants to take in the rays. Maude turns to Mercy, face wet.

"She's alive. Your mom is alive."

Chapter 10

"When people talk about the worst ways to die it's always so basic. Sharks—You're scared of a big goldfish? Plane crash—I'm more scared of flying coach. Buried alive is a big one, but at least you get some solitude for once. Good time to reflect." Mercy sips water and steps back to the microphone. "For me, I just don't want to die of natural causes. So boring. I like a little surprise with my death. Plus, that's not even a real medical diagnosis. Natural causes means you're supposed to die because you're too old and everyone agrees. My great-grandmother was a hundred and three years old, so natural causes. But natural causes should extend to other stages of life. A nineteen-year-old frat boy dies black-out drunk in the trunk of a Toyota Camry with duct tape over his genitals after his frat brothers forgot to release him before March Break in Cabo. For a frat guy, that's natural causes. Thirty-year-old yoga instructor killed by botulism after consuming a bad batch of Kombucha? Natural causes. Fifty-year-old divorced dad bled out from a genital shaving injury hours before a Tinder date with a woman half his age? Natural causes."

Being back on stage gives Mercy a few minutes not

to think about the fact that our mom is still alive and on garbage duty in a Wellspring prison camp. It ain't easy, so she's been taking as much stage time as she can to occupy her mind. Can't blame her.

Dee hacked the site that posted the leaked video and scrubbed through all the footage available but only found that one short clip. Just a woman with circular puffs of hair lugging bags of garbage outside and then pausing to take in the sunshine with a big smile on her face. It's a smile so big that it's like she's smelling rose petals and not the trash she seems to be dumping. And she's extending her arms out to the sky as if the sun is beaming down on her, but Dee let Mercy know that the video was definitely shot at night. And yes, maybe she was staring up at the moon, but it really looked like our mom is taking in the sunshine.

"Different religions have different definitions of hell, and some are nastier than others. You expect a sadistic hell from Christians, especially Catholics. They might just reassign a bad person to a different parish, as they do. But the Buddhists—they're so peaceful, right? The Middle Way. The fat laughing Buddha. If there's hell it must be an over-packed yoga class. The kale smoothie machine isn't working. Nope. Turns out Buddhists are serious about hell. Their hell has six realms. Five wasn't enough. One is called the Realm of The Hungry Ghost, and in that realm your belly is huge, but you have a pinhole mouth and a thin neck so you're always hungry. But if you try to stuff food down it turns to, get this: fire and knives. Sadistic. Suddenly it's like, Buddha, are you laughing as an expression of enlightenment or because you're super evil and love to be creative in your application of terminal pain?"

The crowd barely claps at that one and Mercy doesn't blame them. Works-in-progress all of it, and that's what midnight spots are for. She's enjoying staying under the radar. Not looking for another mainstage disaster anytime soon, not that Lou is about to offer one. For now, it's about the writing, and Mercy's been scribbling jokes on any napkin she can find, trying to build up a ten-minute set. She's even let herself dream of booking that elusive half-hour Special once everything tides over.

Mercy thanks the crowd and hands the mic back to Azeem. She grabs her new backpack (no more canvas bag!) and is heading towards Lou to grab her much-needed clean fifteen bucks when a tall, bougie woman with long blonde hair and designer glasses stops her. She's prettier than the usual open mic attendee, and she's got this expensive-looking purse strap that celebs don online.

"I liked your set," the woman says.

"Did you see it?" Mercy asks, taken aback.

"Can I buy you a drink?" she asks, and now Mercy doesn't know where this is headed.

"Bit of a rush," Mercy lies. She does have a date with Nick who promised they could watch a *Bachelor In Paradise* marathon until dawn, so it's not a lie.

"I'm Cat White," the woman says. "I do development at Comedy Ale. I want to talk to you about an opportunity that might really work for you."

Mercy is so taken aback she goes full Yoda, "Listening. I. Am."

Cat gives her a weird look. "Star Wars, right?"

"No. I mean, yes. I mean… Comedy Ale, you said?"

"We're doing a competition and I'm recruiting talent," she says.

"Talent?" Mercy sweeps her arm around like it's the last thing she'll find here.

"We need different types—up-and-comers who aren't signed to agencies. We already have frat boys comics, feminists, political anarchists, fat, thin, Trans.

But what we don't have, Mercy, is you."

"Who am I?" Mercy asks, genuinely interested.

"You're morbid as hell." Cat White laughs. "Totally obsessed with death. You hardly veer from the subject. How much time on death do you have?"

"About a zillion hours, polished."

"Great. You'll need all of it. We're doing a pretty loose format. You'll be performing material but also might be doing some writing on the spot. It'll be a blast, and you'll get big exposure."

Mercy looks at this woman and this strange opportunity and is understandably skeptical. Plus, she knows it's not possible. Two weeks ago, Mercy left two dead bodies in a casino penthouse. Cops are still looking for who did that. Not to mention that Fanny is still out there, probably ready to out her as a killer when the best opportunity presents itself to save her own ass.

"Look I really appreciate you thinking of me," Mercy says. "But I don't think it's the right time."

Cat White cocks her head like she's trying to understand what would motivate Mercy to turn down the most significant break of their life. "You don't have to be nervous," she says. "I know you're ready for this."

"It's not that. I can't leave my job."

"At the museum? I'm sure they can give you a couple of days," she says, and Mercy can't believe that this woman knows where she works. "That's all it is. Forty-eight hours max. You'd be one of our only open mic finds, which is a big deal. And once you get TV and digital exposure, you'll be fighting off mainstage opportunities. I guarantee it."

"It's not that—"

"—And the prize. I mean the money's not great, admittedly. But what comic would pass up an opportunity to perform in a venue like that?" When

Mercy's face is blank, Cat White acts like it's crazy she hasn't heard. "You really don't know? The top three comics get to perform at The Wellspring. They've built a state-of-the-art performance space. You'll be booked for years just doing material on what it's like inside. The government is looking to soften their image, so you'll need to sign an NDA, but they're going to let a crew inside. With an audience of The Glorious Uninsured." She gives Mercy a long look but then gives up with a shrug. "Oh well, I tried. Nice to meet you, Mercy Gorrison."

"I'm in!" Mercy blurts out. "I mean, I'm definitely in. If you still want me? Yes. Definitely into it and very available."

Cat White pulls out a card and hands it to Mercy. "Text me and I'll send you all the info and a contract. Pack for two nights. We'll put you in a nice residence with the other comics."

"Thank you," Mercy says, overwhelmed.

"See you there, Mercy Gorrison." Then Cat White walks off.

Mercy stands there for a while, stunned stupid. Then she whispers, "Hold on, Mom. I'm coming for you."

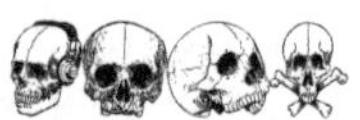

Call time for Comedy Ale's "Comedy Showdown Live" is 7 p.m. in the city. The studio is at the famous Kingsman Market in the hip part of town along the East River. Mercy walks from the train station with Nan's old suitcase, knowing little-to-nothing more than what Cat White told her at the club. This might all turn out to be some prank for all she knows, and that would be humiliating. But the distant chance that she could get into the Wellspring and see Mom again is too tempting to pass up. If our Mom's alive, Mercy needs to try.

The sun sets blood orange above the old converted buildings and glimmers off the river. Mercy stands on the bridge drinking it in. "A delicate sorbet," her mind blurts as a description and she realizes that if "delicate sorbet" is what her brain is serving up, she's screwed in this competition. But as the city winds down, Mercy does feel a flicker of hope. She worked hard to get here—that's not magic, it's what corporate folks call 'sweat equity.'

"Just stay focused," Nick shoved that into her cranium. "Don't forget that you're doing art. Share the art." How a Dogman knows how to give a comedian a pep talk she'll never know, but he killed it. Nick seemed more excited than her, actually, and maybe even more nervous. "Do it again," he said, listening to Mercy's set for an umpteenth time. They stayed up all night. Mercy read him jokes she'd written years before, some on scrunched up post-it notes with smudged ink. They got rid of a bunch. Nick helped her expand some ideas, even wrote some tags. "If you get famous and forget all about me, consider all of my lines about death my murder confession."

"Woah, dark. You're learning."

And of course, Nan and Maude spent days preparing for Mercy's journey as if she'd be gone several months and not a couple of days max. Maude knit a ski sweater with little skulls and crossbones, and Mercy will probably never take that off even though it's well over eighty degrees outside out. Nan baked up a box of cauliflower-based sweets. Gus and Dee, who have become inseparable since they met, came by to wish Mercy luck and sandwiched her with a hug. All that love. If she's ever going to be ready, it's now.

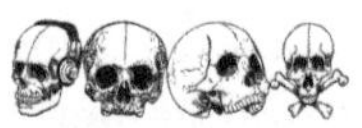

Still, Mercy's legs are jelly when she finally arrives at the address, a converted Nabisco factory, all hipstered up to be a TV studio. Everything's brushed steel and beams; a coffee shop selling tonic water espressos for twelve bucks in the lobby. There's a guy with a clipboard and a walkie talkie checking people in at the elevators.

"Who's your agent?" he asks Mercy.

"The other comics have agents?"

He rolls his eyes, so Mercy points out her name out on the list, and after verifying ID he lets her in. "Elevator to the third floor. There'll be someone up there to take your bags." And when Mercy says, "Gucci." He replies, "Don't do that."

Waiting at the elevator is a short woman and two tall guys, all with bags. The short woman has pigtails with overdone red lips, librarian glasses, purple suspenders, and red Converse. She wears a pin that says, "99 problems and the white heteronormative patriarchy is all of them." Mercy is immediately into it. The other two guys look tired or stoned, but they definitely forgot to shave. Both wear jeans and flannel shirts, and when one says, "You got the flannel memo?" The other one laughs hard until it becomes clear that he's fake laughing and the other guy says, "Dick!" and they both laugh and give each other bro bumps.

The girl with the librarian glasses shoots Mercy an eye roll. "Welcome to the loser's club."

When Mercy looks confused, she says. "Un-agented, right? The big shot comics with reps take the luxury elevator on the left. Apparently, there's champagne and lobster rolls. We take this elevator, which apparently never arrives."

"Lobster rolls?" one of the bros says. "I just came in

my pants."

"I have a feeling that happens to you a lot," says the girl, sharply.

"Woah, sick burn!" the other bro says.

When the tiny elevator finally arrives, they crowd in. Mercy worries that her cauliflower snacks are going to smell up the space and is about to apologize when a hand stops the elevator door as it's about to close and Colby Foster appears. "Oops, sorry… a case of premature evacuation," he says, and Mercy winces at the on-demand pun. "Well, if it isn't Mercy Gorrison. Are you here for… did they… ?"

"I got a call, too, yeah, Colby."

"Wow. I mean, I thought this was only for mainstagers. But great." Colby smiles, looks at the other comics. "Careful of this one. She does death jokes—and you know what Freud said—"

"Freud is the kingmaker of misogyny," the girl with the suspenders cuts in.

Colby is taken aback.

"Duuude, you've already offended the feminist and you just got here," one of the bros say.

Colby reddens, and the rest of the slow elevator ride is in silence.

"I'm Mercy," she offers the girl her hand.

"Sara with an X," she replies. "Welcome to the shitshow."

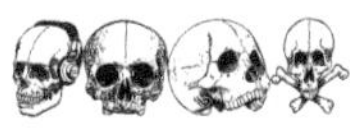

When the door opens, they walk into a large dark studio with a well-lit stage surrounded by cameras. There are bleachers for about a hundred people, where Sara with an X, Colby, the Bros, and Mercy take a seat with about sixty others. A tall guy wearing a Comedy

Ale hat comes out and tells them to simmer down because there's some major nervous comedian energy manifesting itself in a symphony of cackling and shifting and coughing.

"Name's Mike," the guy says. "I'm your producer. You have a question, or want to know where the bathroom is, ask Mike."

"Mike, where's the bathroom? I have to poop," a lanky comedian says, and Mike and the rest of the comics roll their eyes. Hunger Games is already happening here, and this idiot just put a bullseye on his back.

"Left of the stage by the emergency exit," says Mike, and then turns his attention to the bigger group. "Under your seat is a clipboard with a non-disclosure agreement. Please sign and hand that back to me."

Pens start scribbling, along with lame jokes about having to sign over your firstborn child. When the comic who asked about the bathroom says that it'll be hard to prove it's his firstborn since his wife will probably cheat on him and the baby will come out Asian, an Asian comic turns to him and says, "And would that be a problem for you?"

"No! Uh, I just… my ex-girlfriend is half-Korean."

Everyone, even Mercy, seems to need to get out last bad jokes. She turns to Sara with an X. "Why is there a non-resuscitation clause in here?"

"Oh, dark. I love dark," Sarah laughs.

"Then we're going to be pals."

"Already are." Sara smiles. "Sorry that I got all agro on your friend in the elevator. I don't usually judge people, but puns? He seems like a total douchebag."

"You have amazing intuition."

"Is it true you only do death jokes?" Sara asks. "I've tried doing death. It builds tension organically. Can I run my one death joke by you? It's a knock-knock joke.

Knock-knock."

"Who's there?"

"The unstoppable march of time slowly guiding us all towards inevitable death." Sara holds up jazz hands. "BFFs?"

"'Til death do us part," Mercy says.

"Great because we're going to be in a sea of bearded bros, and we should look out for each other. Oh, and did I tell you I need to win this competition? I literally can't pay rent. I just checked my savings account, and it says sixty-nine dollars." They look at each other and yell, "Sixty-nine!" in exaggerated bro imitation, and high five. The bros look over both amused and uncomfortable.

The Producer with the headset gathers the sheets and counts them. "All right everybody, thanks for being part of the show. You're all here because you are some of the best comics in the city, the country, and possibly the galaxy, so give yourself a round of applause. The goal here is for us to give you a prize that has never been given before: A paid gig to perform at The Wellspring. To get there you'll compete against each other in a format that has also never been done before. It all takes place live, in twenty-four hours. If you're lucky, you'll go on stage many times during those twenty-four hours in head-to-head bouts until you reach the end. But if you are eliminated in any of your bouts, it's just like the playoffs: you're out and you'll have to watch the other comics from a hotel room where you'll stay until the competition is over. If you win, you keep going until the finals. And those finals will take place tomorrow night. That final round will be on live primetime TV for the nation to see. It's the reason this show is called *The Twenty-Fourth Hour*. The first twenty-three hours will be telecast online for live polling and then that twenty-fourth will be streamed live on Comedy Ale. So, who's ready to make history?"

Chapter 11

Stage lights come on and also brighten the bleachers where the comics sit. Cameras point their way and it's clear that what happens in the bleachers will also be part of the show. An enormous digital stage clock is lowered that counts back from 24 hours. 23:59, 23:58, 23:57… All the comedians are adrenalized to realize that the competition has already begun, live for the online world to witness, and every move they make is being recorded and scrutinized.

The Host, a veteran comic named Tess Love, gets up on stage and the cameras swirl around her. "Ladies and Gentlemen, welcome to the Twenty-Fourth Hour on Comedy Ale. This is the first comedy competition that takes place live in a twenty-four-hour period, and you get to decide who wins in real-time. I imagine the folks looking for comedy at this hour are pretty savvy, a bunch of Einsteins, so I'm not going to explain anymore. Let's get started, shall we? The first round is called 'Two Mics.' Each comic gets to do one minute of clean material, and then they must switch to the other mic and do another minute of filthy, dirty humor. Anything goes, but it's instant death if you drop the N-word and you're not black. I will make sure of it. Online viewers, your live votes will determine if a comic stays in the competition or if they are instantly eliminated. So, let's go, right? Woot?"

"Woot!" the comics cry out.

"First two comics up on stage are… Chad Hayhurst and Sara with an X! Wait-wait, what kind of name is Sara with an X? That some kind of Malcolm X thing? She better be black… where she at?"

"It's Sara Whithaneski. It's a Jewish thing," Sara calls out from the bleachers, and already people are laughing.

Tess Love wipes her brow, and that gets a laugh too. "Okay, Sara and Chad. Get up here and do some live ass comedy!"

Turns out Chad is one of the frat bros in plaid from the elevator. He makes a show of twisting his baseball cap backward in homage to Sylvester Stallone's cheesy 1980's arm wrestling movie *Over The Top*, and only the bros laugh. Sara is up first at the clean mic and Mercy is nervous for her.

"People talk about cultural appropriation," Sara begins. "Some of it I get. Like when you see a white person is driving badly and you're like, 'hey, that's an Asian thing!' But cultural appropriation is easy to miss when it's not about your culture. Like, as a white person when I'm called out for being a mumble rapper with over eighty-one Spotify followers, I'm like, but I love rap. I was brought up on Drake. It's my love language. How is it my fault I'm influenced by it? That would be like criticizing a highway rest stop for being into kinky sex. It's just what it's been exposed to. But recently I read an article about Klezmer music, which is an ancient Yiddish folk music played by Ashkenazi Jews of Eastern Europe. The report said that in Germany, non-Jewish Germans are dressing up like Chassidic Jews and dancing around to Klezmer at bars. As a Jew to that I'm like, that's some cultural appropriation bullshit. Stop it! Stop it now y'all, or I'm gonna to mumble rap on yo' ass! If you want the fun, Klezmer-part of being Jewish you have to also accept the large-segment-of-your-extended-family-being-exterminated part of being Jewish too."

Sara's first minute is up so the Frat boy steps on stage and takes over. "We've gotten so used to apps solving our problems. Hungry? Takeout.com. Lost? Google Maps. No cabs? Uber. But what about a scenario where you have to get rid of a dead body? Your hooker overdoses, and you're like… Uber Corpse! Fuck, it's Mardi Gras, weekend prices are surging. Who can pay rates this high? Just don't do Uber Pool mode. You don't want your hooker corpse mixing with some old grandma's body. That's just gross!"

Tess Love comes up when he's done, "Uh, that's the clean mic bro. Dead hookers? Ah, we'll take it, this if for the internet! Okay, time to hit the dirty mic."

Chad goes all-in on dick jokes. "I was thinking about how Magic Johnson was a great basketball player but with that name he would have been a much better porn star. But then again, the rest of his Lakers also had great porn names. James Worthy… of vagina. Kareem Abdul-Jabbar is so easily turned into Cream Abdul-Jabbar…"

Mercy hates to admit it but those are precisely the kind of dumb jokes that people love online. But when Sara steps to the mic, she takes a more direct route.

"CUNT!" she shouts. "Cuuuunt. Cunt. Cunt. Cunt. Cunt," she says over and over, and then she sings it, like in a sad opera. "Cuuuuuunt. Cuuuuunt." And then with a country twang, before finally ending with, "I cuuuuunt beat Chad Cuntface over there without your cunty online votes, so vote for me, ya cunts!" Sara bows and hands the mic back to Tess Love.

The votes are live on a big screen next to the stage

and Sara beats Chad by a healthy margin. Tess Love walks Chad's suitcase onstage. Chad is expecting a nice little goodbye ceremony, but costumed security guards rush the stage and push Chad off while Sara with an X celebrates, dancing with Tess Love. It's their signature elimination segment. You're out with your bags while the person who defeats you gets to dance. For the comics watching this unceremonious elimination from the stands, it's like blood is in the water. Everyone starts eyeing each other, wondering how to destroy the person who moments ago they were paling around with, maybe even helping out with tags for their jokes.

Sara is out of breath when she sits down next to Mercy. She guzzles tea from a pink enviro-mug as if she's just come from a feminist UFC cage match, which she basically has.

"You're my hero," Mercy tells her.

"No time for that. I saw the list and you're next up." Mercy gulps, and suddenly Sara is like Rocky's trainer. "I learned a few things up there, so listen up. They seem to want to throw you off since there's a monitor that shows you a mirror of yourself with the live polling, as you speak. It's emotional fucking torture, and I barely held it together. You need to stay focused on the camera above the screen. Do not under any circumstances look at the reflection of yourself. Don't do it. Oh, and don't forget that the only thing the internet love more than dirty shit is dark shit. So this challenge is made for you. Go dark-dark."

Tess Love is back on stage "Up next, Mercy Gorrison up against… Dave Apples?" Even Tess Love seems surprised by the name she just read off the monitor. A wave of murmurs comes over the crowd of comedians, and Mercy goes pale.

"Did she just say Dave Apples?"

"This is some bullshit," someone from the bleachers

says. "That guy had a sitcom."

Mercy knows that well. We used to sneak into the den at night and watch re-runs of "Bad Apples" with the volume low enough that Mom and Dad wouldn't catch us. It only lasted two seasons before a series of drunk driving arrests got him cancelled, and we moved on to "Modern Family."

Dave Apples walks in from backstage. Was he given his own green room? Those famous bright blue eyes sparkle under the stage lights, and his cocky grin is cockier than ever. He provides the crowd with a modest, gee-shucks wave.

Sara grabs Mercy by the shoulders. "Listen to me, Mercy. You've got this. You've got to forget all of the lights, all of the cameras and Dave fucking Apples, and you just go and take this. You're my only friend here." Sara squeezes her arm. "Take it."

"Take it!" Mercy repeats, but then walks to the stage on wobbly legs.

"They put me up against an open mic'er?" Dave Apple gives Mercy a smug up and down. "Jesus Christ, how the mighty have fallen. What's next, a baby?"

Apples shakes his head, and they both step onto center stage. The lights are far too bright for Mercy. She catches a glimpse of the camera set-up, and seeing herself on the screen sends shivers down her spine. Thankfully, Tess Love calls Dave Apples up first, and he struts onstage like a peacock. He's still got that perfect lightly greased hair that always falls on his forehead, making him have to brush it back, which he does to punctuate punchlines. It's a euphemism in stand-up circles for using a physical tick to punctuate a joke. "Pull a Dave Apples," people have said since before Mercy started doing comedy. And now she's about to go head-to-head with the man himself.

"At least you'll have time to watch some good TV

from your hotel room," a lighting guy says to Mercy. Mercy flips him the finger, and the camera catches that.

Dave Apples grabs the microphone as though it's the keys to his Tesla.

"Women put so much emphasis on feelings," he begins. "Had a fight with my girlfriend. She thought I was being patronizing. I said, 'Do you even know what patronizing means?' She said, 'But these are my feelings. I need you to validate my feelings.' And I said 'just because you feel something doesn't make it true. Hitler had feelings that he should kill the Jews. Do I have to validate his feelings and have my sister-in-law Rachel die in a concentration camp?' She thought about that and said, 'Yes.' It was such an insane but stick-to-your-guns response that I didn't know whether to run or propose right then and there. So, the wedding's set for August..."

It's an old bit that everyone recognizes, but the crowd of comics don't seem to mind, and that's not helping Mercy's confidence. Apples waves to the camera like a pro. Like the camera is his pal. When the MC calls "Mercy Gorrison," it's like she's hearing someone else's name. She takes a deep breath through her nose and walks out there since what choice is there? Mercy sees Sara with an X in the crowd, and she motions for her to keep her chin up.

"Sometimes, I'm a bit too much in my own head," Mercy manages to say into the mic. "This morning I was crossing the street and there was a crossing guard and I said 'morning' like you're supposed to. And then I was like, 'You idiot you left out *good*. You just said *morning*.' He probably thinks you think he doesn't know what time of day it is, and you just wanted to point that out. You patronizing jerk! He knows what time of day it is. The guy's probably a high school graduate. You're probably racist too. He looks vaguely Mediterranean.

Screw you!' And by that point, I've been standing in the middle of the street and cars are honking and the crossing guard says, and I swear this is true, "Move along, lady. Like you said, it's morning."

Mercy gets medium chuckles and makes the huge mistake of looking at the online votes that appear like a heart monitor under the camera. It's middling at best. She walks offstage, and Dave Apples is waiting.

He scoffs. "Wow, okay. Crossing guard joke. Are you sure?"

Sara comes running and pulls Mercy away from Apples. "Mercy, what the hell was that?"

"What?"

"You're the death girl. You do comedy about death?"

"I was trying something different."

"Not the time to try something different." Sara has an urgency in her voice that actually frightens Mercy. "You want to lose to this idiot? Do death. And you better do it dirty as hell. Because right now you're getting your ass kicked, and that shithead is going to be dancing around the stage."

Mercy knows she's right. The online polls are up, side by side, and after that first round they are so heavily in Dave Apples' favor that he's now laughing openly. Tess Love gets up again and says it's time for the Dirty Mic. Dave Apples struts on stage again and bows slightly as he takes the mic. There's a mischievous glint in his eyes, and he walks right up to the camera, super-close up as if he's telling the audience a secret.

"Hey, so given the scores in the first round, it's mathematically impossible for Crossing Guard Girl to beat me. So let me just say this, thanks, and see you in the next round, fuckers!"

Apples blows a kiss to the cameras, then drops the mic on the floor before he walks off the stage. He still has time left, and the stage just remains empty as the clock ticks. But he's cackling with laughter along with the cameraman who is loving the footage. And then with ten seconds left, Apples walks back on stage, nudges the mic off the stage with his foot and walks off again, cackling. It's a huge dis to Mercy, and everyone knows it.

Tess Love motions for Mercy to step to the Dirty Mic. Even she looks uneasy. Mercy looks out at Sara, who gives an encouraging nod. She puts out claws, and mouths, "Death."

Mercy glances offstage with a smile, pretending like she's sharing an "lol, you got me!" with Apples. She picks up the microphone off the floor and gives it a pop to make sure it's not damaged.

"If I asked you to guess the most dangerous threat to American civilization, you'd say what, North Korea? Gun violence? President McCabe gets a Tik Tok account?" Mercy looks at the monitor and sees that the mention of the President gets a little bump in voting. "Nope. America's most dangerous epidemic is actually men trying to be deep. People maybe like Dave Apples over there. That's the scourge. Dave, never try being deep, okay? Keep it light like you do because the alternative is catastrophe. Ever heard a guy like Dave Apples talk about death? Nine out of ten times how do they want to die? Having sex. They're like, 'I want to finish and just keel over like—blaaw.' Sounds deep—go out doing what you love? Fair. Except here's what that looks like from my perspective. First, if you're the type of guy who's about to drop dead during sex I'm not picturing Liam Hemsworth. I'm thinking, well, Dave Apples. Old and gross. So clearly I'm nowhere near getting off, and Dave finishes way too fast and then collapses on me, maybe spitting blood or even vomit on my face. Probably shits himself? Been known to happen when a washed-up sitcom star dies. Very likely to happen to Dave Apples over there. So I've got this flabby, hairy, cold, dead has-been suffocating me in a soup of puke and blood and cum and shit, and I'm gasping for breath struggling to get out from under there. And then what—gotta call the cops, right? There's been the death of an old washed-up white dude with a failed sitcom. But here's the thing, he died in my shitty rent-controlled apartment in a bad neighborhood, so the cops aren't exactly offering condolences. I'm dealing with a murder rap. And you know what? That old balding halitosis motherfucker got me pregnant. Blaaw!" And then Mercy drops the mic. If she's going out at least show people she tried.

The cameras follow her to the bleachers where Sara runs over and hugs her. "Fucking killed it!"

There's a lot of confusion as the online polls come in, and producers run all over the place. In the stands, comics start speculating that there's a Wi-Fi problem. Finally, Tess Love calls Mercy and Dave Apples back on stage, and Mercy is more than ready to be rushed out by security and into the comfort of a hotel room. At least she can sleep.

"We've got a mathematical unicorn," Tess Love says, "An exact tie!"

"What? Bullshit!" Dave Apples says.

"Yup. It's a tie, Ladies and Beta Gentlemen," Tess Love confirms. She takes both of their hands and raises them in the air. The security guards do a bit where they don't know what to do and one of them carries the other offstage. Dave Apples forces a smile like this is all silly but when they're offstage, he corners Mercy.

"I didn't even bring out my new stuff. Just drudged up some old, tired bit. Which is to say you got very fucking lucky. Don't fuck with me again, understand?"

Mercy can't help but look at his face—that famous face with the impossibly bright blue eyes and greasy hair, but she can see wrinkles coming in, cracks in the armor. "I've frightened you, Dave Apples."

Apples glares at her like he's going to explode or strike, which will not go well for anyone, when Sara buts in. "Fuck off, Apples. She's with me."

Apples looks at Sara like he wants to rip her head off too, but his face turns red and he just stomps off. In seconds he's on a cell phone screaming at his agent.

"That's what success looks like," Sara says, with a wry grin. "Proud of you, Sis."

"Thanks. I thought I was a goner."

"Well, don't rest. They're making us live Tweet through everyone's set. It's joke stealing at the highest level."

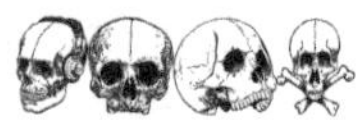

They tried to kill Mercy off up by putting her against Dave Apples, but she wasn't the only one to be fed to the sharks. Soon it becomes clear who are the predators and who the chum, as they pit comics who are "similar" against each other, thereby getting rid of perceived doubles. Two Hispanic females. Two deadpan comics. And then of course, two Punsters.

Colby is called up against Jesper Van-Sheriden, three-time Punderdome champ. Colby goes pale when he takes the stage next to his idol, and Mercy watches him shake as he steps to the mic. "The periodic table has been around for one hundred and sixty-five years. That's a long time for something that is around only periodically," he begins. That gets a laugh, not as much as he's used to, but not bad. "I'm so OCD, but I call it CDO because I need all of the letters in order."

Maybe Mercy is getting a soft spot for the guy because she actually laughs at that one, and gets nervous when

Colby moves to the dirty mic since no one's ever heard him say so much as a dirty word in all his time on stage. He looks deeply uncomfortable.

"It was probably especially hard for Jewish people with ADHD to survive in a concentration camp."

The place lights up with groans but also laughter. Mercy can't help but Tweet that Hilarity Hut Pun Legend Colby Foster does it again with a Holocaust joke! When Jesper Van-Sheriden comes up, he gets medium applause for a joke about a how 'The person who coined the term 'coined the term' really coined the shit out of that term.' It's a joke the crowd knows from the internet, and Van-Sheridan must have forgotten that he's in a room full of comedians who despise joke stealing much more that they do Holocaust jokes. When the votes come in Colby wins. Mercy runs up and hugs him, and the camera follow.

"But I thought you hate me?" Colby asks.

"I don't hate you, Colby Foster. Your puns, they're nothing short of voluminous."

Colby tilts his head to the camera for the absolutely unavoidable retort: "Voluminous?" he repeats. "Coming from you, that means *a lot*."

When the camera leaves, Colby is stunned. "Did you just set me up for a pun to camera?"

"I did," Mercy shrugs.

"Friends for life?"

The rankings come out after the first round of eliminations. Out of the sixty-two comics who showed up thirty-one are left. Sarah is in eighth place. Colby nineteenth. And even though Mercy tied the famous headliner David Apples they have her in dead last place, thirty-first. The deadpan comic ranked thirtieth looks over at Mercy, "You suck."

Chapter 12

The next round, they stick with the Two Mics theme but this time it's Political and Apolitical. Dave Apples is up first against the comic who told Mercy she sucks. Apples must have pulled some strings with his agent to match up against the comic who (other than Mercy) is in last place.

Apples pulls out a classic bit that only die-hard fans have heard, "I don't have a problem with global warming lefties. I have a problem with some of the dumbest people I know pretending to be Harvard climatologists every time Global Warming is brought up. 'According to NASA, Greenland lost two-hundred and eight-sixty billion tons of ice since 1993.' Dude, I've known you ten years and all you've talked about is Xbox and pussy. He was at my place, drank five beer cans, crinkled them up and threw them in the trash. Then I'm washing dishes and I leave the water on for five seconds and he's like, 'Duuuude, polar bears need that!' Before that the only time I heard him mention the planet was when he was trying to figure out if he could smoke weed out of it."

Mr. Deadpan breaks out this lukewarm joke, "The Feds raised the interest rates again, making it hard for banks to find loan applicants. As incentive, banks are now offering home loans with free lawn signs announcing 'Foreclosure.'"

Apples swaggers to the Non-Political mic. "When you pick up your dog's poop you're doing the exact opposite of what your dog wants. Poop is its only means of communication with the outside world. It's their one phone call from prison. And the message is always the same: 'Save me!' Because dogs are our prisoners. We tell them when to eat, where to go, where to hide the shiv in the common showers after they've taken out a gang rival. It would be like if you were on a desert island, put a message in a bottle and God picked it out of the ocean tossed it in the trash and said with a smile, 'Yes, you're a good human. Good human!'

Two solid bits, and Apples actually points to Mercy in the crowd when he walks off stage as if to say, 'That could have been you.' Sara was right though, Mercy rattled him.

All Mr. Deadpan musters in response is another flop, "Amazon delivery is getting pretty fast. Yesterday I ordered a pair of gloves and the by the time I pressed 'Buy Now' I was wearing them."

Apples wins by a considerable margin.

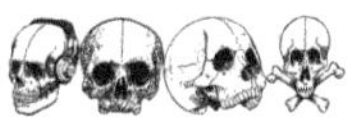

Other comics go on, and of course Sara kills again, starting at the Political mic. "There should be a video game called 'Moral High Ground' where the goal is to hunt down opportunities to take the moral high ground. Like you track down someone and say, "Oh, you're going on a vacation in Israel, huh? During Nakba? Oh, you don't know what that is? Didn't think so. It's a day of protest for the Palestinian people memorializing their displacement. But I'm sure you'll enjoy your falafel sandwich while watching starving children beg for work permits at the border.' Achievement unlocked! And then you get double points for telling someone to check their privilege. Because nothing feels cozier than slipping into a nice warm bed of moral superiority. Oh, you're getting married? A cis-gender wedding? Whatever, I only go to double Trans weddings where both people are A-sexual and don't even want to do it, but that's just me. You do you. Achievement unlocked!"

Her opponent, a nerdy absurdist comic does okay with, "Congress is pressuring for a ban on Tik Tok, which they call a Chinese propaganda app. As a daily user I disagree. This is just another example of rabid American Imperialism and capitalist war-mongering aggression! Fuck America!"

Sara moves to the next mic. "I visited a really pretentious bookstore. Know how I know it was pretentious? I asked the guy at the front desk where the Humor section is. He frowned and said, 'We don't have humor here.' I was like, oh… so you're kind of like Dave Apples?"

There are "Oohs" and "Damns," from the crowd, but mostly laughter. Her opponent's retort earns groans: "Coffee's getting a bit fancy isn't it? This morning I bought a latte, and it came with a certificate of authenticity."

Sara moves on.

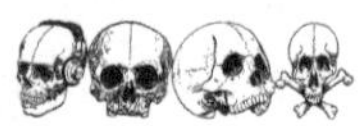

There's a break after the first few comics and a producer approaches Mercy. "They want you in the interview chair."

Mercy gets jealous side-eyes from several other

comics and a thumbs-up from Sara as she's led out of the stands and into a small lit room with a green screen and a plastic chair. They touch her up with powder to make her forehead less oily. A female producer named Suzie sits left of the camera. She's wearing a Comedy Ale baseball cap, a hoodie and a forced smile. She tells Mercy to respond to her not the camera. "So, how's it going out there?" Suzie asks.

"There's a lot of talented comedians," Mercy says. "I'm just thrilled to be competing."

"Huh, okay," the producer says, not masking her disappointment. "In the first round you went up against Dave Apples. What was that like?"

"He's a seasoned comic. Has a good following. Have to respect that. So…"

"Hold up," the producer says, and the sound guy and cameraman go slack. Mercy has clearly done something very wrong.

"Look Mercy, I shouldn't be telling you this, but Dave Apples just sat in that chair and trashed you to high heavens. We all had to sit through him calling you a talentless hack, and have been seething about it. He called you, and I quote 'an open mic whore who got lucky.' So, can we cut the pleasantries? This is a cutthroat competition with a ton at stake—a prize that will make the winning comics famous. You're not going to win any friends playing the middle of the road."

"Got it."

"Good, because there are a ton of other comics dying for a sit-down."

"I said I got it."

"Great." The producer forces another smile. "Why don't you tell me about your feelings about Dave Apples?"

"Dave Apples is a douche towel with a scabby micro-penis," Mercy says, and smiles fill the room. "I intend to eliminate his hairy, pimply graying ass from this competition and possibly from life. He thinks I got lucky, but he got lucky with his stale bit from twenty years ago when he was last relevant." Even Mercy is surprised by her venom.

"There she goes!" The producer winks. "You've been branded The Death Comic. So give me more of that flavor."

"I'm Comedy's Angel of Death and I'm coming for you, Dave Apples. I'm going to riddle your body with a blizzard of punchlines, then bury you deep under the stage where you belong," Mercy says.

The producer grins. "Is that a threat?"

"That's a direct threat, Apples. I'm going to murder you on the internet for everyone to see. Apples will rot!"

"Ha—say #ApplesWillRot."

"#ApplesWillRot," Mercy says. "These Apples are way past their expiration date. Disposing of them is the act of compassion that the public have been yearning for and I'm here to help. In fact, I'm here to put down any comic who is secretly in pain and praying to be put out of their misery." She stares at the camera. "#MercyKills."

The interviewer's eyes widen in bliss. "That's going viral! Oh my God I'm so excited. Okay. Now tell me your plans for this next round?"

"I'm going to murder anyone who steps in my way."

"Great!" The producer smiles. "So let's really get into your dark brand of humor. Why do you have such an obsession with death?"

Mercy likes this question. "Death is the punch line to every joke. We laugh because we're all going to die in the end. Because life is a theatre of the absurd. And everything that happens is just—"

"That's interesting," the producer cuts in. "But this

will cut fast. We've got your philosophy covered. So let's get into you as a person. What happened in your life to give you this dark perspective?"

"Just born morbid. My baby gift was a death rattle."

"Ha, I hear a memoir title!" the producer says, but Mercy can tell she's faking enthusiasm. "But seriously. You've had some trauma in your life that really gave you an insight into it. Your mother and father?"

Mercy gives her a blank look. "What about them?"

The producer looks down at her sheet. "They died in front of your eyes? And your bother…"

"Ha, no, my parents live in New Jersey. Retired. I guess you could call that a kind of death," Mercy says, trying to turn it around.

"You were nine years old," the producer continues. "You watched as your father was shot and your sick mother was dragged off to The Wellspring—she was terminal. Did our fact-checkers get that wrong?"

Sweat slithers down Mercy's back. The producer leans in, somehow going from hard-edge reporter to old friend. "Mercy, I know I'm going to sound like a sleazy producer here, but a sad origin story helps." She sighs. "Look, I understand if this is too hard for you."

"No, I'm good. I can talk."

"Good. Then please walk us through what happened; about the day your parents left you."

Mercy's jaw feels frozen, her eyes sizzle, but she pushes it out. "I was nine. My brother went to boarding school, my mother was sick and Uninsured. The van came and my father fought back and… there was a gun. He was shot, My mother was taken…"

"This happened right in front of your eyes?"

"Everything was taken from me," Mercy says, and tears stream down her face.

"Who took it from you? Who changed your life when you were just a child?"

"The Wellspring."

"Say that in a sentence."

"The Wellspring took everything from me. Ruined my life." The producer just looks at her, and in that silence, Mercy finds herself saying. "I want to see my family again."

"But you know that's not possible?" the producer asks. "Tell me that."

"I'll never see my parents again. Or my brother."

"Good, Mercy. That is tragic. You must have a lot of anger towards those responsible for taking your family away. If you could be in a room with the President McCabe right now, what would you say?"

Mercy imagines being in a room alone with the Plastic President, her straight blonde hair and perfect smoky eyes, and she's got her sword out. That's what she'd do. Terrify her the way she did our family and then slice her head clean off her body. "I'd get her on a stage, and then..." Mercy is about to admit to everything about the process at Curated Ends, go into detail, when the interview door opens, and Mike the Producer enters.

"We need the comic back up in five," he says.

Suzie looks so pissed she almost throws something at Mike. The break in tension gives Mercy a moment to collect herself and breathe, thank God. When the producer looks at Mercy again she can tell that she's lost her. "Thank you for that, Mercy. We got everything we need. Good luck out there."

The audio guy is already changing batteries and everyone in the room turns away as if Mercy is already gone. She stands up and lets Mike the Producer hustle her back to the bleachers.

"You're up in three minutes. So stay here," he says.

Mercy sits, clenching her jaw so as not to cry again, but she completely loses it. She hasn't spoken about what happened to her parents aloud, well, ever, and it all flashes in her mind—the ice cream cone, the van, the dog, Dad struggling, Mom coughing, the bodies, the screams. Tears stream down her face and she's aware that the cameras are on her. They're getting a nice comedian meltdown. Sara runs over and moves Mercy behind a pillar where the cameras can't get a clean shot.

"What the hell did those skeevy producers do to you back there?"

"Nothing… I'm fine."

"Did you tell them anything? You didn't admit anything, did you?"

"What would I admit?"

Sara looks both ways. "I'm telling this you because we're friends. There's a rumor going around. A bad one. They say you work in the curated death business. That you kill. Like actually kill." Sara looks Mercy in the eyes. "I don't care if it's true, okay? Actually, I think you're a fucking hero if it is. Fucking Wellspring. But it's starting to all make sense. Your focus on death. It's your subject matter but also your job. I know this is crazy, Mercy, but everyone's really excited by what you might say up there."

"Up where?" Mercy had entirely forgotten about the competition. Mike ducks around the pillar and gives Mercy a one-minute sign. Sara grabs her shoulders.

"You want to win this, Mercy? You want to go to the Wellspring?"

"More than anything."

"Then get up on that stage and go raw. Give that crowd of internet trolls a piece of yourself. A pound of flesh. Do you understand me, Mercy?"

"Gorrison, you're up," the producer says.

"Show the world who Mercy Gorrison really is," Sara says. "Fuck 'em all, right?"

"Fuck 'em all," Mercy replies.

She heads over to the stage and everything glimmers. If the comics are gossiping that Mercy works in curated death, it's only a matter of time before the cops piece it together and they have her. Life in prison. Nan and Maude Uninsured, and once the Dogmen return they're off to The Wellspring too. At least Mercy knows that this is how her story ends. She kept it under the radar because she's a failure of a comic and no one noticed, but now that she's on camera, she's practically waving a flag for the cops.

And perhaps my sister Mercy's imminent end focuses her mind because she has a singular focus as she walks onstage. The comic she's pitted against, a tattooed rocker-type, smiles widely to the camera, but then his smile fades as he passes her. He winks. "No pressure, Killer."

Mercy steps towards the non-political microphone first, but then does something she hadn't planned. She drags that mic over to the other microphone, the Political one, and make them one. The mics screech of course, so she turns one off.

"Breaking all sorts of rules doing this. But yolo, right?" Mercy gives the producers the finger as a crowd-pleaser. She gazes out at the screen and can feel the people online watching her. Alone in dark rooms, off long commutes from mindless jobs, or somewhere hiding like she's always been. Are they judging her? Yes. Like Sara said, they want their pound of flesh. Entertain them or be gone, life's hard enough.

"I'm a Wellspring orphan," Mercy begins. "Both my parents were taken. My mother was terminal. She was dragged onto one of those scary black vans. Why's it always got to be a black van, right? Seems a little racial. Couldn't go for lemon-colored?" That joke gets a little nudge in online polling, so she's encouraged. "My dad tried to protect her, and they shot him. And they say chivalry's dead. Nope, just my dad." Another polling bump. "Happened right in front of my eyes when I was nine years old. I mean, couldn't they have waited till I was a teenager, so I could've hated my parents already? Nope, nine years old—when your parents are your idols. Anyway, I hid behind a garbage can like a coward and watched it all go down. I remember licking the soft-serve ice cream cone that my previously-alive parents had just bought me while it happened. Even as my mom screamed my name at the top of her lungs and the van drove off to who-knows-where and I became orphaned, I licked the ice cream. The lesson here is that soft-serve ice cream is so delicious that even the death of both of your parents won't cause a pause in licking. Soft serve is so good that it looks like a poop emoji, and we still eat it. That's how much we love soft serve. And it got me thinking that if those black vans from The Wellspring sold soft serve out the side window people would willfully go. It would be, 'Wait, you're going to take me away from my family forever to a mysterious quarantine that evokes Nazi Germany? Um… can you do a twist with chocolate sprinkles?'"

That gets a laugh from the crowd, but at the side of the stage there's restlessness. The producers argue about whether to stop her. Tess Love doesn't know which way to go.

Mercy continues, "But that's why we're all here, right? The government is so good at publicity they're getting us comfortable with the notion of the Wellspring as a prize. Free comedy show! Look how open we are! Try our soft serve ice cream! I mean, look at this—they've got us competing to go there now. What's next, scratch and wins?"

A producer waves at Mercy from the side of the stage trying to stop her, but it's too late.

"The President claims it's all about transparency—

she wants us to see what a nice life she's curated for our Uninsured sick. Chick-Fil-A on Sundays. Netflix is free, and you don't even have to share a password! We're all here as part of the President's PR narrative, everyone here, everyone watching. Yes, even you online-weirdos masturbating to this right now. The same message has been beaten into us for years: Insured people are good, Uninsured are bad. Insured are like the popular kids in high school who made student council. The Uninsured are the goths smoking cigarettes on the library steps." Mercy looks out to the crowd of comics. "You sir, with the neck tattoo. You look Uninsured. I mean, lip piercing? Who are you kidding?"

Instead of answering, the comic hides his face behind his hoodie and waves her off.

"I don't blame you, buddy. They might come for you next. But the message is on repeat: The Insured planned right, worked for it. Uninsured: idiots, illegal immigrants, murderers, the unlucky, guys with neck tattoos. We deserve it. Want to avoid being one of those folks? Go to college, they say, you'll get full insurance there. Can't afford tuition? Student loans! Sure, you'll graduate with crippling debt but there will be a corporate job waiting for you with benefits because God forbid you want to work a job that helps the world. Classic American trap—keep the people busy paying off debt so they're too busy to change things. But something has changed. Now even regular soul-sucking corporate jobs don't offer full health insurance. You have to earn health credits, and those don't come close to covering you if something disastrous happens, like if, say, you've got a bottle of Grey Goose stuck inside you? Or have a pre-condition like… a bottle of Grey Goose that has always been stuck inside you? Forget about it. And if you just have something weird like a third nipple? Sorry. If you want to be fully Insured and safe from The Wellspring you better get one of those high up super-soul-sucking executive gigs, so better start climbing, triple-nipple-guy. And don't dare slip and suffer a broken leg because we don't cover that. Talk about a trap!" Then Mercy goes there, because it's the only place left. "No wonder people are lining up for curated deaths." Mercy can hear rustling of paper as the producer who interviewed her steps into view giving her a 'cut it off' motion. "It's not because the Uninsured want fantasy deaths, like they say on TV. It's just affordable. And the prospect of dying in The Wellspring is more terrifying than dying on your own terms. Does the President know that? You have to imagine that she does. But it may be the only thing she knows other than how to get that smoky eye look."

Another laugh, another polling bump.

"People say my comedy is dark. That I'm obsessed with death, but my mind just goes there. I'd love to just be obsessed with sex—that would be so much easier and way more fun. But what's darker than living in a country where the government lets you bleed out in the streets if you don't have a glowing green triangle in your wrist? My mother was a fighter. And if she were alive, she'd say 'burn it all down.' She might also say, 'Are you wearing clean underwear?' But burn it all down and start over because this system is broken. The powerful have us trapped and distracted and we're too scared to fight back. But we have to fight back right now or risk losing everything. So Mom, I hope you hear me up there. And you people watching—even you, creepy masturbating guy—I hope you can do something because it's up to you to rise up and fight this government and its whole rigged system and burn it all down. Burn it down! Burn it down! Burn it down! Burn it all down to the ground! But when you do, can you please leave some soft serve ice cream?"

Mercy drops the mic on the floor. There's a screech and then more silence as she slumps off stage. Mercy walks by Sara, who looks the other way. She takes off her glasses and folds them as if she never needed them in the first place.

Dave Apples snickers as Mercy walks past. "No one will remember your name in a few hours, and you can go back to your sick, twisted life, Psycho."

The camera is on them, so Mercy gives one last immature nugget, "Dave Apples, you irrelevant sitcom reject. Write a new joke or just die in a drunk driving accident already." Then she walks off towards the exit.

Tess Love is back on stage, a bit frantic. "Ladies and gentlemen. According to the rules, the last comic will be docked twenty percent of her online votes for combining mics. That's not okay, apparently. Now, onto the next comic…"

I bet my sister Mercy is thinking, "Ha, twenty percent of zero? Who cares!" She takes the elevator down and walks outside into the dawn light, completely forgetting her suitcase. The sky is baby blue with soft clouds. Gorgeous. There's a slight hum to the city, and a slow rhythm of street sweepers and grocery workers pulling boxes off trucks. Mercy's not even sure what the hell just happened in there. She feels great pride and deep-seated dread. This is definitely it for her as a comic, she figures, possible as a free citizen, but no one can say she didn't go for it. Maybe she should start a podcast?

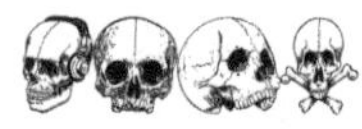

One of the street sweepers gives Mercy a wave as she walks by. Then a small crew of workers gathered around a cell phone in front of a frozen meat truck wave as well.

"Hey, you're that comic," one of them says.

"I guess," Mercy says, not even sure anymore.

"You told those phony motherfuckers what's what. Hey, can I get a selfie?"

"Yeah, that was some brave shit. Don't ever stop being funny, okay? We need it."

Mercy smiles and poses with the guys. "Thanks."

Encouragement of any kind is catnip to a stand-up comic, especially to a struggling one, and as Mercy walks off she starts to wonder if maybe she can organize an open mic night of her own. Might have to be from in prison, but she could move up to MC. Mercy finds herself skipping over puddles by the end of the block, almost dancing. She looks up at the beautiful sky and thanks God for the beauty of the world and all of the weird opportunities, when wheels screech and a black van blocks her way. The door swings open and two SWAT cops and a Dogman leap out. This has happened to Mercy before, so she enacts the glowing green triangle on her wrist and hold it up for them.

"Insured and healthy," Mercy says. "You gentlemen can relax."

They grab her by the shoulders.

"I said I'm Insured! I'm Insured!" Mercy screams, hoping the workers will hear and run to her aid. But she's pulled into the van roughly and a hood blinds her. She hits the metal floor hard and is held down by her neck. Her heart pounds. She feels a sharp pain in her leg, and screams but can't help but think: *This is what Mom experienced…*

And then she feels weirdly happy for a moment before everything gets woozy.

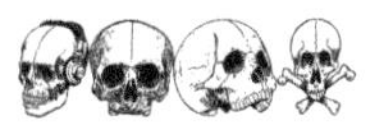

Mercy wakes in darkness. She tries to move but is tied down to a cold metal chair. Her hands are cuffed behind her back. Feet are cuffed too. There's a pain in her spine that she can't reach. It burns and stabs. She struggles but can't get free, so she tries to breathe through it. "I said I'm Insured," she mumbles, but sound barely comes out. Her hood comes off and darkness turns to shocking fluorescent light. The room is white and windowless. Everything is blurry, but there's someone in there with her, a SWAT guard with a gun strapped to his chest and a visor over his face. Mercy wonders if he's protecting her or protecting others from her.

"Where am?" she ask the guard. But he stays quiet, face forward, so she yells, "I said, where the fuck I am, man?!"

The guard flips up his visor and his eyes are red and full of rage, and Mercy knows she's made a massive mistake because he's on her in a second, hands around her neck. Mercy's eyes burn, and she can't breathe. She feels herself dying. The soldier raises a gloved fist and Mercy braces for impact.

"Stand down! Stand down, soldier!" The SWAT guard winces, fist midair. He's been interrupted murdering Mercy and he's pissed. His fist lowers but his other hand stays clenched around Mercy's neck. He turns that into a finger that he pushes into her face, like a warning. "I said stand down!" the voice orders again.

The guard finally releases Mercy's neck and she crumbles, gasping for breath and coughing. "Report to Terminal Five," the soldier is told, and Mercy recognizes that it's a woman's voice speaking that is vaguely familiar. "Get some water in here."

Mercy's head is still lowered so she has no idea who's in the room now or how many people have witnessed the assault, and if there will be more to come. She opens her wet eyes and tries to focus. In front of her is a woman with slicked-back hair and a face full of make-up. She's small and corporate in a blue business suit—real OCD type. Mercy tries to piece together what department of what agency she may have pissed off to earn a visit from her, and that's when Mercy loses her breath realizing who this slick corporate woman is.

"Hello, Mercy," says Sara with an X. Even her voice is different. Sharper now. Gone are the colorful suspenders, dorky glasses, and feminist majority pin. "Apologies for that." A new guard walks in with a plastic cup of water. "Remove her restraints." He does, and Mercy is so relieved to get out of the cuffs that she forgets to lunge forward and murder this woman for tricking her.

"I knew you were a phony," Mercy lies, once she's done drinking the water.

"Really?" Sara with an X pulls out a phone and plays Mercy a recording of her own voice admitting that she works in curated death. "You go confessing murder to phonies all of the time?" She then opens a laptop on the table. It's the Comedy Ale sit-down interview. Mercy's first thought is 'those bastards did a horrible job with makeup. Skin is oily as hell.' Sara plays the clip of Mercy telling the world that she's going to murder Dave Apples. "That's enough to put you away for years, right there."

"Reality TV is considered hard evidence these days?" Mercy asks. "The Kardashians should be on death row."

"Perhaps it was just a joke," the woman continues. "But you were so quick to spill the beans. We just didn't think you'd spill the whole jar. A full-on confession on a live stream? Not even letting the cops do their job."

"Your jokes were terrible," Mercy says. "You're a

hack."

"My joke writers would be so disappointed to hear that. They were expensive. But you are funny, Mercy, all on your own. And now the whole world knows it. You've become a bit of an internet darling, actually. But don't get it twisted. If you never return to the public eye no one will care. If you die of suicide in this room no one will ever miss you. You're a confessed killer. You left the competition, overdosed, no big deal." Sara with an X pulls out a large yellow pill. "Consume this and it's all over. And don't worry, we'll help you swallow it. We'll just need you to write your suicide note."

"You'll have to talk to my agent about written work," Mercy says.

"Funny. I'm impressed with your poise. Then again, you're the famous Ninja Girl. You don't fear death, you probably welcome it." She shakes her head. "No, suicide would be too easy. But you're going to give us what we want eventually, Mercy. So enjoy your prompting."

Sara with an X folds her laptop and walks out of the room, and two masked guards enter, including the one who strangled her.

The hood goes back on.

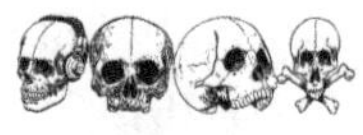

President McCabe likes to brag that her state-sanctioned police interrogation program is "so much better than some other countries." Maybe you've heard her talk about it on the news, cozy at home with a glass of Pinot. If my interrogation was any comparison, then here's what happened to my little sister Mercy that day. They strapped her to a table. Choked her. Electrocuted her through her feet and fingers. Put pressure on her eyeballs until they almost burst like grapes. Brought her pain in ways she never imagined. Made her hurt until she felt like she was going to die. Until she hoped to die. And by the time they were done—when they dumped her crumpled body off on the very street corner where they nabbed her, part of Mercy was indeed dead—the part that was soft and naïve, the part that slept.

But like with me, they didn't kill all of her.

And that was their biggest mistake.

Chapter 13

Mercy staggers home in the darkness. Her pants urine-stained, fingernails aching, and her spine burning. They took her cell phone, so there goes Uber. The streets are abandoned like there's some kind of elevated military curfew. When she finally reaches Cedarville Apartments it's like a mirage; a swim-up bar in the Sahara. The elevator is broken again. So slowly, painfully, she drags her body up the nine flights of stairs, unlatches the locks and falls flat onto the floor inside. She's on all fours crawling to her bedroom when she looks up and sees a tableau of some of the people whose lives she's surely ruined with her stupidity and pride: Nan, Maude, Dee, Gus, and Nick too. They all gaze down at her in horror like she's a ghost. Then they lift her gently off the ground and carry her to bed.

Sleep is filled with horrifying nightmares. Acid thrown in Mercy's face. Animals chasing her with knives. Mercy twitches and screams and fades back to sleep for more hell.

When she finally wakes, it's light out and only Nick is in the room, scrolling his laptop.

"How long have I been out?" Mercy asks, her voice sandpaper.

"Two days," Nick says, his face pinched with concern.

Maude enters with Nan and Dee. "How is she?"

"Sweetheart, thank heavens," Nan says. "We thought it was a coma."

"And you didn't take me to the hospital?" Mercy asks.

To that question, Nan looks away. "Want some pineapple juice?"

Mercy takes a sip, but she doesn't like Nan's reaction to her question. She looks down at her wrist and presses. The triangle that has glowed green all of her life does not show up. In its place, a red rectangle. Uninsured.

"You too?" she asks Nana and Maude, who nod sadly. Mercy tries to move but there's soreness everywhere. She looks at Nan and feels so sad. "The competition was all a scam. And now I've ruined everything. I'm such an idiot." She begins to cry.

Weirdly, Dee is grinning. "Can you still tell jokes?" she asks.

"I just told you what I've done." Mercy sniffles. "Jokes are beside the point."

Nick turns his laptop. An article reads: "*Dark Web unmasks comedian as President's Spy.*" And there she is in the photo: Sarah with an X. The red glasses and suspenders next to a photo of the slick businesswoman who interrogated Mercy nearly to death.

"It's a huge embarrassment to the government that they infiltrated their own competition with a fake comic," Nick explains. "The President tried to spin it but now she's distancing herself from the whole thing. Called this woman a rogue agent with artistic ambitions and arrested her."

Dee grabs the laptop and continues reading, "With the President's spy eliminated from the competition, her spot was given to the comedian with the highest online polling in a single round, known as The People's Choice." Dee's face looks crazy. "That comic is Mercy Gorrison."

"You're going to The Wellspring," Nick says.

"You must have questions?"

But Mercy only has one, and she goes full Southern Belle to ask it: "Whatever shall I wear?"

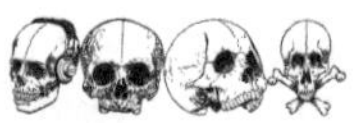

Orientation begins a week later. A car picks Mercy up and drops her at a blocky gray building downtown. She lugs her overnight bag through a metal detector and past security guards who frisk her as if she's entering a prison. This building must have been a hospital at some point. The halls are cold and sterile with metal bars along the walls, possibly to help former patients walk. Next to the elevators is a framed poster touting The Wellspring's passive-aggressive mantra: "Heal with discretion."

I remember when the Vogovin Virus hit and hospitals like this became overwhelmed. No one knew what the Virus was or how to treat it—people just started dying. My boarding school went on lockdown, and you couldn't cross state lines so there was no way home. They didn't even let us call home because the government wanted to control the flow of information, worried that it was some kind of enemy attack. Back then, President Phyllis McCabe was just another tech billionaire from Silicon Valley whose daddy was CEO. But when her own brother Teddy got sick, McCabe took family money to create a secret quarantine out in the Northern Woods. After Teddy died, rumors of the research being done there on human subjects ranged from unethical to worse. Eventually, her team of scientists walked out with a cure. A simple injection that wiped Vogovin off the map.

"I cured the world," McCabe loved to brag on TV. It was her crown jewel. A treatment that worked in hours and saved hundreds of thousands of lives. Of course, McCabe's corporation had a patent on the cure and through private enterprise she made billions more, which is how she managed to keep the facility open even after Vogovin was eradicated. And then, voted in as President on the wave of her heroics, Phyllis McCabe kept it running for our "Glorious Uninsured" under a shroud of secrecy that only she has the power to enforce. That secret quarantine was rebranded as the "The Wellspring" around when it took in our mother and killed our father, and it's remained a black box ever since, with President Phyllis McCabe as its benevolent guardian. And now, thousands of other Wellsprings are on the way. Being built across the country like a franchise. All will tout the same message: Trust in Her. Fear Her. The Wellspring will Save. The Wellspring will Heal. Heal with Discretion.

Mercy finds Room 11 at the end of a long hall. It's a spacious classroom with a podium set before a dozen rows of chairs. About forty people mill around, and they all look like artists. A circle of guys with spiky hair and leather jackets surround guitar cases and a drum kit. A dozen Asian men and women in colorful athletic clothes do pirouettes. A magician shuffles a deck of cards and freaks out a tall girl leaning against a unicycle. And then there's Mercy's group, specifically, the other two winning comics from the Comedy Ale competition: The Pun-meister extraordinaire Colby Foster, and of course, that bloated, blue-eyes wonder, Dave Apples.

"Well, if it isn't the replacement comic?" Apples gives a slow clap as Mercy enters. "Between you and lowest-form-of-comedy-guy over here, guess I'm the headliner."

Mercy glances at Colby, eager to set him up. "Has he been harassing you this whole time?"

"He *has-been*," Colby replies.

They both look at Dave Apples and burst out laughing. When Apples realizes he's being pun-roasted, he turns bright red and storms off. "Ah, you can both go blow yourselves!"

"So glad you're here, Mercy." Colby smiles. "Apples was starting to rub off on me."

"So, this is it, huh?" Mercy asks, looking around the room. "Send in the clowns?"

"You think they're really going to take us into The Wellspring?" Colby asks. "I mean, this isn't some scam where we're going to perform in front of a green screen and then be held at gunpoint to tell the world how wonderful it is?"

"I had no idea you had an ounce of cynicism in you," Mercy says.

"Puns are just my comment on how limited our language is to express the truth about humanity and death," Colby says, but then grins. "I'm just messing with you. I'm so excited I couldn't sleep. I heard we get free t-shirts!"

A man in a dark suit with enormous gray eyebrows and a thick mustache walks up to the podium and taps the microphone. "Jake Bearden, Chief Communication Strategist," he says in a voice so monotone that the comedians crack up, assuming it's a bit. But it's not. Bearden looks down at his clipboard and only glances up to be disappointed by what he sees before him. "Congratulations on being selected to entertain the glorious people of the Wellspring. The government has been fully transparent about the top-shelf Health Care we offer to our nation's Uninsured sick. It is so open, in fact, that we are peeling back the curtain further to entertainers like you. From this moment on you are ambassadors to the government and represent the President in everything you do. You have all signed NDAs, so legally you may not mention anything that happens from the moment you entered this building onward or risk jail time and financial punishments. Clear?" He looks out to the audience with a stern look. "I'll need a verbal on that."

Awkwardly, they all say "sure."

Bearden taps his clipboard like he can't wait to get out of there. "Let's keep it on the straight and narrow, folks. I expect you to be on your best behavior, following directions, especially when you're on stage doing your thing. Whatever your thing is…" He rolls his eyes, only imagining. "We leave in twenty minutes. Bathroom visits are recommended now—it will be a long ride."

"At least it won't be a wide ride," Colby jokes.

"Good idea about taking a crap before we go," Dave Apples says, appearing again. "I've got about thirty-six in the chamber, and I ain't Wu-Tang if you know what I mean." Colby and Mercy just turn away, and that infuriates Dave Apples more. "I was trying to connect with you losers!"

"I'm not Wu-Tang either." Mercy winks to Colby. "Be right back."

She walks off to the bathroom and enters a stall. There, Mercy retrieves the tiny earpiece that Dee custom-created for her trip. Like the one from the Gabiglia Casino, it's disguised as a tiny mole and even has a hair poking out of it for maximum "stealth and verisimilitude." Dee fixed it to Mercy's thigh for entry into the building so Mercy carefully pulls it off onto her fingernail and sets it on the edge of her ear, as instructed.

"Oh good, toilet paper," she say out loud.

And when she does, Dee's voice rings out loud and clear in her ear. "Copy that Mercy. If you hear me say the second code word."

"I do love soft toilet paper."

"We're in!" Dee says. Mercy can hear Nan and Maude cheer in the background. Dee grabs the microphone close. "Now remember Mercy, you're going to want to talk to me. But I can hear well. Frankly, I can practically smell it." Mercy cracks up when she says that and then realizes what she's doing. "Stop reacting. We talked about this. Ears are everywhere. I stay silent, you stay silent. I can hear your conversations. And if there's an emergency, code word is vampire-sixty-nine."

"They'll never suspect a thing," Mercy says.

"Stop talking," Dee repeats, so Mercy just coughs.

It's hard to pee with an audience, so Mercy just flushes and stands up. When she gets out of the stall one of the Asian dancers is staring at her.

"Just practicing my set," Mercy says, lamely. The woman rolls her eyes and turns to wash her hands. "What are you, like an acrobat?" The dancer dries her hands methodically, gives Mercy another suspicious look, and walks out without saying a word. "Crap," Dee says as if she's actually in Mercy's brain and not just in her ear.

When Mercy returns, the group is already being led out by Borden. She follows them down to a parking garage where a tour bus is waiting. The musicians load their gear, and the rest of them head into a luxury Greyhound with the softest seats Mercy has ever felt. It's dark and cozy in there. Mellow classical music plays from the speakers. As the bus begins to move, the windows frost and then black-out entirely as if they've been painted over. You can't see a thing even pressing your face to the glass, which Mercy does. She looks over at Colby and he appears as skeptical as she does, but no one else seems to care. They settle in, maybe eager to get some shut-eye. The lights dim until it's almost completely dark—the bus is a calm little pod.

"The windows are blacked out," Mercy whispers for Dee's sake.

"No shit, Sherlock," Dave Apples says from two seats away, and Mercy realizes that she really has to watch herself.

The Asian gymnast from the bathroom rises from the seat in front of her, frowning. "You talk too much," she says.

Mercy is about to give her the finger but worries that she'll point her out to security or maybe she's security herself, so she just lets it pass and slides back down into her comfy seat.

Of course, no one knows where The Wellspring is or how long it will take to get there. That's a national secret that's never been breached. Once the bus gets moving, it goes fast, and though it's hard to perceive just how fast, the smoothness of the ride makes Mercy think that they're on some kind of private highway. No stops, no slowdowns. For hours it's like they're on rails. Eventually, the lights on the bus darken completely and people start to nod off.

"Yeah, like we're going to be able to nap. We're going to the goddamn Wellspring, right?" Mercy says to Colby.

But Colby's already asleep, and Mercy's eyelids feel heavy like weighted blankets. A pleasant mist falls lightly on her skin, which nudges her further into the best nap ever. Mercy fights it, but the embrace of sleep is too enticing, and a little sleep might help her performance. Mercy closes her eyes and it's like she's carried off by a family of swans. Her dreams swirl purple, shape-shifting like the Northern lights. Then it's a lush rainforest, tropical birds, sloths hanging lazily from tree branches. Deep green moss feels soft underfoot, making her bounce and even fly. Mercy dreams and giggles, but at some point she realizes that it's just a dream and wakes up, but the lull of sleep is too powerful and pulls her back in. She repositions and rolls back into the lush, mossy rainforest in her imagination.

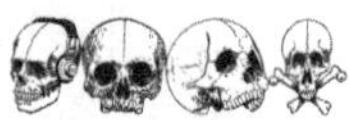

When my sister Mercy wakes again the lights are on in the bus and everyone is gathering their bags. How long she slept she has no idea, but it could have been an entire night.

"How long was I out?" Mercy says aloud.

"Twelve and a half full hours," Dee says in her ear and Mercy is startled—she'd totally forgotten about the earpiece. "Luckily, you snore like a bear or else I would have thought you were dead."

Mercy looks up and the Asian woman from the bathroom is glaring at her again. "You talk too-too much."

"Yeah, we covered that. I'm a regular blabbermouth."

The bus slows to a crawl and when it comes to a full stop, there's silence onboard. They all act casual and line up to disembark but everyone is aware of the gravity of the moment. They're about to see it. The first non-Sick civilians, as far as anyone knows, to see The Wellspring. The musicians trail out first, then the magician and juggler, the group of dancers, and finally the comedians.

"What in fuck's hell?" Dave Apples asks.

What appears before them is an assault on the senses, and Apple's vocabulary doesn't suffice to describe it any better. The first thing Mercy sees is deep green moss stretching out along a black tarmac. "Stretching out," because the moss actively grows before her eyes. Two blocky gray buildings with industrial chimneys appear ahead, but the moss climbs that structure too, softening the concrete with green. Moss grows beneath Mercy's feet, expanding like it's alive, and a lush, rainforest expands around them as if it's reclaiming the land from the dank industrial city in real-time. Tropical birds twirl in a blue sky that has gorgeous wisps of clouds. A babbling brook stretches off in the distance, and the sound of rushing water soothes. Mercy realizes that this is similar to her dream, and that's when her vision shifts back—as if the frequency of a radio station flickered to a crappy station, and suddenly she sees all of the industrial grayness around her again and the rainforest recedes. It's a bleak pale sky again, blocky buildings, ugly smokestacks coughing from long chimneys. No green at all, nor tropical birds. But then her vision shifts back again—and the buildings, the chimneys, all of it, is now lovely growing green moss and the rainforest is now bigger than before, the dead gray sky a softer baby blue, and the colorful birds twirl now in unison as if to show off. Beauty becomes more defined after the glitch, as if autocorrecting from Mercy's imagination.

"Are you seeing this?" Apples asks.

"A pony farm!" Cody blurts out, eyes wide with wonder.

"What? No, you idiot. The NASCAR track," Apples says. "Is that Dale Earnhardt Jr.? He's back from the dead?"

"You don't see a mossy rainforest?" Mercy says.

"What the hell are you going on about, Psycho?" Apples asks. "Are you both dumb? And I'm being rhetorical in case you can't tell!"

They all look around in wonder but it's clear that not

one of them is seeing the same thing. Borden, with his raincloud eyebrows, appears before them. For Mercy he is framed by a rainforest mirage; for Colby maybe a pony farm; for Apples perhaps Borden stands at the starting line of a NASCAR racetrack; and who knows where for the others? For Mercy, Borden himself is left unchanged and is clear as day but what's around him keeps shifting. The forest blinks to a deeper green, breaks for milliseconds back into bleak grayness, only to transform again— lusher, fuller greener—adjusting, always adjusting like a website with struggling Wi-Fi. A family of deer ambles out into the open field, but after a flicker Mercy sees masked guards with guns strapped to their chests. She tries to hold onto the image of the guards, but the deer return more detailed now, horned stags; elegantly they amble along the mossy ground. They tilt their heads, eyeing her curiously.

"Don't fight it," Borden says, as if there's a megaphone in Mercy's thoughts. "You are experiencing a comforting reality—your favorite reality of what The Wellspring should be. Let it ease in because that really is The Wellspring. It will comfort you for as long as you are here. Should only take a minute for your brain to accept it wholly, and then all you'll see here are teddy bears and rainbows, or whatever you love to see most. It's your Wellspring. Everyone's Wellspring. Curated for personal comfort."

"How does this happen?" Colby asks, innocently enough.

"Simple, really," Bolden answers. "While you slept you ingested a viral influencer mist. No harmful side effects. The mist simply encourages your brain to see what you want to see most. To strive for the pleasant. It will reverse itself by the time you get back on the bus with an antidote mist. But until then, enjoy it. It won't affect your performance on stage, we've tested that. Some performers actually prefer it since they can conjure up their notes to concentrate better. Other than that, you'll see what you want to see: an appreciative crowd, a standing ovation, whatever appeals."

"What if we want to see the real Wellspring?" the female Chinese dancer asks. Mercy is now sure she's a spy. Who would have the guts to ask such a brazen question?

"This is the real Wellspring, Ms. Ping," Borden says with a dark smirk. "How real you want it to be is really up to you. Now please, follow me."

Borden leads the group towards a large building in the distance. Mercy knows in her heart that it's ugly and gray with steel bars on the windows, but what she's seeing is a charming medieval castle overtaken by vines like something out of The Hobbit. Mercy even starts to feel the soft push of moss beneath her feet, even though she knows that the path is paved slick and gray like in an airport hangar.

"It's beautifully green, but before it was like an industrial parking lot," Mercy says aloud, and as she accepts it verbally her vision gets even more green, more lush, the sound of chirping tropical birds louder and more pleasant.

"I read about this mist-based viral influencer on the dark web," Dee says in Mercy's earpiece. "You can fight it, Mercy. When you have a chance, I want you to close your eyes. Close your eyes hard and try to see what you saw when you first walked out of the bus. Hold onto that image, that reality, and try to paint it back into your mind with all the details you remember. That image is your only chance to be awake in the real world, or at least in what is closest to reality. You'll never see what's really there until the influencer wears off, but you can see something more real if your mind summons it. The more your imagination fills in a world from fantasy, the faster the influencer takes hold. So you have to fight it, Mercy. Fight it. Do you hear me, Mercy? Fight it!"

Mercy closes her eyes and tries to summon the bleakness of what she witnessed before her vision blipped. The armed guards. The smoke-filled chimneys, the gray sky and bleak tarmac. She paints an image of drabness and fills it in. Grips onto that reality. And as she walks, the softness underfoot hardens again, and though she still hears tweeting birds, she can discern churning machines, the roar of distant trucks as well. The sweet smell of fresh moss is mixed with metallic smokestacks and a thick, oily taste. When Mercy opens her eyes again there is still a forest, still moss, but now everything is in black and white like she's watching an old film. Two deer run through the field in front of her, but when she focuses it's armed guards walking lock-step with machine guns. The group arrives at the building's front door, and the colorful toucan that hovers above Mercy's head becomes a black drone, beeping instead of chirping, watching her every move.

"They have unicorns!" Colby delights, but Mercy can see that they are just two more armed guards waving them in.

"Stay focused. Blend in," Dee repeats.

The others smile and gawk, enjoying the wonder of their imaginations, so Mercy matches their dreamy smiles. But she holds onto the gray city that twitches in front of her. She closes her eyes as if inhaling pure bliss but again builds, builds, builds the world that is true, that doesn't make sense to her eyes. That she knows is real. Inside the building, soldiers with deer heads and human bodies are posted along the wall, gripping machine guns. Mercy closes her eyes and sees that they are just masked SWAT men. There are Dogmen in there too with their German Shepherds, which were totally invisible to Mercy before. The Dogmen make her think of Nick. He said he'd be with Dee at the apartment when she left, but Mercy hasn't heard him in the background. She feels a jolt of anxiety that she never asked where he was and why he wasn't there. Mercy find herself hoping that Nan feeds him something other than cauliflower snacks, and that's when Mercy realize that she's totally gaga in love with this guy and that she'd better get out of this place alive or risk never seeing him again.

The group is led into a bright, sterile room and told to strip naked. Of course, everyone dances out of their clothes like they're about to jump into a hot tub at the Bellagio. Mercy does the same but can see the soldiers with their rubber gloves and prods, and it's harder to smile. She pretends it tickles when they prod her toes and comb through her hair and spread her butt cheeks open. She giggles more when they look into her ears, hopeful that they won't look too closely at Dee's mole and find her out. They grab her neck to steady her and peer into each ear with a flashlight, but they are fooled. The dancers all prance a bit as they put back on their clothes (maybe they already see the stage?).

Mercy does her best to laugh— comedians do that. And laughing lets her close her eyes undetected as she tries to keep the world around her real. Borden does the final inspection. He has a flashlight, and peers into each of their eyes, presumably to make sure they're fully gone, brainwashed by this viral influencer. Mercy smiles as she peeks down the row. Borden is having a hard time inspecting the musician's eyes because they keep air drumming and air guitar-ing. The dancers do pliés, which frustrates Ol' Eyebrows even more. When he gets to Colby and shines a light in his eyes, Colby says, "I'm feeling a bit light-headed." Borden rolls his eyes and heads to Mercy. He holds her chin roughly and points a light directly into her eyes. She tries to zone out, give the thousand-yard stare, but Borden quickly drops the flashlight and Mercy realizes that she's done for.

"Her." Borden motions to the guards and two of them grab Mercy.

She tries to squirm, but they hold her tightly and walk her out into the hall and to another smaller room with a glass encasement in the center, like a massive upside-down vase. The guards push her into the encasement and the glass closes over her. A reddish mist sprays on Mercy from all directions. She closes her eyes hard, trying to fight it. Borden knocks on the glass.

"Who taught you to fight it?" he asks. "The Resistance?"

Mercy opens her eyes to respond but Borden is a beautiful horned deer with comically bushy eyebrows blossoming with flowers. She keeps trying to fight it like Dee said, and she sees Borden again for a quick second with his horrible eyebrows and mustache and dark suit, but it's harder to hold onto.

"Oh, deer, oh deer. Pretty antlers." Mercy chuckles.

Borden's not buying it. He puts on a health mask and enters the glass enclosure. He looks around Mercy's face. Pulls at her skin, sticks his fingers in her ears. And that's when, totally by accident from what she can tell, Borden drags his finger along Dee's microphone-mole. It comes out of Mercy's ear, and the adhesive sticks onto Borden's fingernail. He doesn't even notice it, but Mercy knows it's not on her anymore, and that Dee is with Borden now. He exits the enclosure and closes the door. Mercy is sprayed again. And again. She feels dizzy. And lovely. Jazz music plays, Thelonious Monk, but then blips for a second and she hears a distant fire alarm.

"The hell's that?" Borden complains. He turns to one of the guards. "Take her to Single F. Watch her till she's nice and gone. I'll find out what's going on."

The guard, who is enormous, grabs Mercy roughly, but it feels soft and loving, like a maternal hug. He drags her down the hall, and the soft, mossy ground gives Mercy a little bounce. She's floating through a lovely rainforest path with colorful birds. Smiling sloths wave at her from the trees. She gives in because why not? Down the hall, children play by a river's edge. They splash water and giggle. The guard shoves Mercy into a cell and closes the door but it's a lush rainforest to Mercy. She sits back and enjoys the florid canopy above. But the guard doesn't leave the room right away. He grabs Mercy by the shoulders and shakes her.

"Keep hold of yourself," the guard says in a heavy Russian accent.

"Vlad?" Mercy smiles broadly, leaning in for a hug. "My friend! Hey, isn't this place rad?"

Vlad places a gloved hand over her mouth. "Shhh!" He flips open his visor, and to Mercy it feels so good to see his deep-set eyes, that bulbous nose, and immovable chin again. "Say nothing. And swallow this." Vlad places an enormous green pill in her mouth, so big that it almost makes her choke. "Twenty minutes, will kick in," Vlad says. "And will hurt. A lot. But you keep smiling. Say nothing. Smile. See The Wellspring they want you to see. But be in reality. Meet you later."

"Hey, where are you going? We can watch toucans together!"

Vlad closes the cell door and Mercy lies down on the soft mossy ground and gazes up at the ceiling in wonder. A fragrant rainforest canopy opens up to a brilliant blue sky. Wispy clouds morph into cartoon faces. Donald Duck sticks out his tongue, Dora the Explorer waves. On a tree branch, a friendly sloth hangs lazily. He blows Mercy a kiss, and Mercy mimics the sloth's movements. He's playfully pulling himself up and then dances slowly along a thick branch. Doing the moonwalk for her. It's hilarious, and Mercy is laughing so hard her abs hurt. But then she sees something crawl onto the sloth's shoulder. It's a big fat spider with hairy legs and eight gleaming red eyes. The sloth doesn't seem to notice it so Mercy points.

"Slothy, slothy—careful. Danger."

She's still laughing as the sloth dances around, whirling his arms, clowning, but the spider rests on the sloth's shoulder ominously. It bares its fangs, which are long and sharp. Terrible like two enormous swords. The spider plunges them into the sloth's neck. Mercy hears a horrible squeal, and the sloth's stunned eyes fill with blood, which drips down onto Mercy's forehead, warm and syrupy. She tries to wipe it away, to summon back the hilarious dancing sloth, but the blood is a faucet and when she wipes it from her eyes she sees the sloth go limp and loosen its grip on the tree. The spider hops off the sloth's shoulder, and the sloths lifeless body falls towards Mercy, landing with a grotesque thump next to her head. Mercy looks over, and the sloth's blood-soaked eyes are open and stunned, its face deranged like it's about to explode with maggots.

Then, another softer thud. This one is more spine-chilling. The spider, big as a catcher's mitt, lands by Mercy's feet. Its wiry legs crawl onto her foot and she is paralyzed with fear. The spider makes its way up her leg and settles on her chest. Mercy's arms are frozen. Her heart pounds under the spider and she gets the feeling that the spider enjoys it—her fear, the thump of pounding blood, like an ass massage for this terrible tarantula. Its fangs come out again. They plunge into Mercy's chest, making her entire body buck with pain. She wants to scream out, but remembers what Vlad said, so she screams into clenched teeth as the spider's poison infects her bloodstream. It begins with an itch, then a burn, until fire seers her veins. The spider grows bigger; red eyes glimmer. It stabs her again. Mercy sees her own bloody flesh fly in the air like tossed salad. The pain is so terrible she convulses. The spider crawls onto her neck now and looks into her eyes, enjoying her pain. And then its eyes flatten and become a TV screen.

"Mercy," the Spider hisses. "Look at me." On the screen is the faces of all of the people that Mercy killed at Curated Ends. The old, the sick, the desperate. They glare at her, their shocked faces miserable as her sword rips through their necks. Dark blood sprays from decapitated heads. "Mercyyyy," the spider repeats, and now its voice changes from a hiss to a more fragile, elderly one. "You disappoint me, Mercy." Ester's voice says. "Your heart is rotten."

"I'm sorry, Ester," Mercy whimpers back.

"Luis would have hated you," Ester says. "I hate you."

The spider holds Mercy's ninja sword in one of its hairy arms. The blade is blood-soaked and singed with fire from the garbage can where Mercy dispensed of it. The spider throws the sword from hand to hand like a baton, toying with it. Then it pulls back and lunges for Mercy's throat. Mercy's head separates from her body and the pain makes her shriek. A guard peers through the slat in her cell door, so Mercy forces a laugh as her severed head bounces feet away from her body. Tears stream down her face, mixing with blood, burning like acid on her skin. Yet Mercy forces laughter through the pain, and slowly, it begins to ease the hell. Each new laugh yanks her lifeless body closer to her severed head, and when her exposed jugular veins meet, they solder together in fire, and the sting is so painful that Mercy screams again, but she does it with laughter, tricking her voice to laugh even as a wound fuses horribly around her neck. A thick scar forms as the spider flickers like a hologram and is suddenly gone, and the moss and the rainforest canopy disappear, the trees too. But not the pain. The pain remains. An intolerable sting, like crushed glass rushing through her veins.

But Mercy is being observed by a guard through the slat in her cell door. So she continues to laugh as if she's heard of the funniest joke of all time. She twists and grinds in the flames that engulf her but laughs as the rainforest evaporates into a tiny white cell with a gray metal door and a flickering red light from a camera above that records every move Mercy makes and all of her laughter, laughter, horrible laughter…

Chapter 14

"What do you see?" Borden shoves Mercy awake. "Where are you, Mercy?"

Mercy forces a smile. "Wonderful Wellspring. Beautiful and green."

Borden points a flashlight in her eyes, and this time even though Mercy sees the horrible situation in all its starkness, she passes his test. Vlad's green pill must have done the job to dilate her pupils in a passable way.

"Good-good," Borden says. "You can see anything you want, Mercy. All of the goodness and wonder. But it's time for you to get on stage. And they're going to love you. But you must change your material, okay? No jokes about death. Not even one. Or else I have to take your sloth away. Do you understand me, Mercy? Not one death joke."

"Only happy jokes," Mercy replies.

"Good. Do those. The crowd will love it. But one mention of death and..." Borden makes a motion to grab something out of the air, and Mercy reacts as if he has her favorite sloth in a chokehold.

"Okay!" Mercy says with a chuckle.

Borden seems satisfied. He walks her out of the cell and down a long hallway, which Mercy pretends is a lush rainforest. She even bounces a little and reaches for the ceiling like there's a toucan above. But the cold prison-like hallway, the solitary confinement cells are clear as day. She's able to peek through some slots on her way past and sees withered people in hospital gowns staring in wonder at the ceilings, poking at the air above them and laughing, tripping balls on the red mist. In some rooms, prisoners moan in pain, but Mercy sees more red mist fall on them and they stop. Time to recharge. Mercy wonders how long the stuff lasts and how (and where) enough of this mist is produced to keep the whole population of Sick high twenty-four-seven? One thing's clear: the government manages to cart out a new, happy Wellspring resident for the Press every few months to describe the wonderful Wellspring. And their joy always seems weirdly genuine. Mercy sees now that it's been mind control all along. The Wellspring drugs the Sick into false joy and compliance. But why? Why not just let them die? And how do they keep them alive for so long if they're sick?

Mercy is hardly able to process her thoughts on that before Borden leads her through a set of secure doors and into a backstage filled with ropes, pulleys and a long velvet curtain. Producers with headsets race around, prepping for the next act. Beyond the curtains is a stage and a crowd of about a thousand. Mercy can hear them roaring with laughter before she can see them, but when she does, it's stark; most are in hospital gowns, except for those in the front section, where patients are dressed up like retirees on vacation. Crane cameras whirl around those folks, focusing on their reaction to what's onstage. And they are delighted by what they see. Mercy watches Colby up there at the microphone.

"I work freelance," Colby says. "Lance is an innocent man!" The laughter is so loud that Colby has to raise his hand to slow the roar for his next pun. "If a stand up comic has the ability to communicate with ghosts, should they be called a comedium?" The crowd roars again, but Mercy notices that it's at an odd moment, an extra beat after Colby's punchline, as if they are not laughing at Colby at all. On the red mist the audience could be laughing at a juggling poodle for all anyone knows. The crane cameras could be flying around like actual cranes. Colby is too far gone in his own dream-state to notice. "Thanks so much. You've been such a grape crowd!"

Colby gets his first-ever standing ovation. He places the microphone back on the stand, takes a bow and skips off stage to thunderous applause. He's so delighted he embraces Mercy, and she sees that his eyes are saucers.

"Mercy, it's so fun out there. They're like pun fanatics. I couldn't miss! You're going to destroy!"

"That's punderful," Mercy says, forcing enthusiasm.

The dancers are on stage next. Even watching them sober, they are impressive. They lift each other into human pyramids, flip in the air and form into impossible shapes. And they smile the entire time. Mercy notices that the woman who called her out on the bus is having a harder time smiling than the others. She wonders if the mist didn't take her fully either, or if she ingested a green pill too somehow. But she performs beautifully. There's a grace to her movements that surpasses the others, and when the dancers form a human pyramid that spells LOVE, the crowd erupts in ear-splitting applause.

After that, and almost as if to test the audience's ability to stay happy no matter what, Dave Apples skulks onstage. He wears his trademark cocky grin, his blue eyes flashing. "I understand women being angry about the airbrushing that goes on in beauty magazines. It puts an unrealistic bar on beauty. That's not what women look like. Women have pores. Actually, in my experience, women look like they've just been crying, but maybe that's just the women I date. But men aren't looking at beauty magazines, ladies, don't stress. We're looking at porn. And porn stars—they really exist! Those women are out there in the wild. Only one alcoholic dad away from taking their spot in the limelight! Do you know how that makes us men feel while we're masturbating?" There is some subdued laughter from the crowd—more than he deserves. Dave grins. "I told that joke at a club, and a guy came up to me and was like dude, that was 'Hitlarious.' Huh? Excuse me? Did you just evoke the great villain of this planet's history to describe my masturbation joke? I'm honored!"

A rumble of laughter takes the crowd, then a blast so loud that you have to wonder what classic George Carlin bit they just witnessed. Even Mercy can't help but feel embarrassed for Dave, whose stale old jokes can't possibly be in the taste of this crowd. Mercy thinks she heard him tell that joke on his first album from twenty years ago.

But it gets worse. Apples goes to maybe his stalest joke ever: his Canadian bit. "Pretty sick of the notion that Canadians are nice. Let me give you a little history lesson in case you didn't win free tickets to see Hamilton. I'm sure you memorized the soundtrack. Remember how Hamilton stole the cannons from the British, and that King sang about using his army to kill the friends and family of the American soldiers? That's the British, right? But where do you think those Brits went to after we started winning? Back to the UK? No, they retreated across enemy lines. To Canada. That's right, Canadians are just British soldiers hoping we didn't notice. And they leave clues everywhere. Ever seen their Monopoly money? The King's on it. The King of England. We had a big war and a lot of folks died. Those 'quote-unquote' nice Canadians burned down our White House. Want to understand what Canada is? Take the drunkest heckling asshole in this place—I see you, there in the blue shirt—and then have a UFC fighter with an AR-15 sit down right next to him and share his table. Suddenly, who's the politest guy in the room—the nicest? That same drunken heckling asshole. I see you, Canada!"

The crowd laughs, but even Dave looks strained, like it was a chore to repeat his oldest bit. And it confuses Mercy. Even on the red mist she wonders how Apples could derive pleasure from repeating that joke? Why not try something new when the audience will fall in love with anything? But something happens at the end of the Canada bit. In the crowd, an old, bald and withered man in a cardigan and thick glasses stands up from his seat. The smile on the man's face is twisted, and he seems to be crying as he's laughing.

Dave Apples turns to him. "Woah, a standing ovation from… wait, there's only one of you. Does that even count? What makes an ovation anyway? You, standing there in the middle of my set. What's your name?"

"Stan," the old man says.

"Of course it is," Apples says. "Stan stands. Stan, huh? That's actually my Dad's name. Or was my dad's name since he's dead. What do you do, Stan?"

"Periodontist."

"Ha, that's so weird because my dad was—" Apples pauses. "Dad?!"

The whole crowd explodes with laughter. It's a solid crowd work bit. Dave laughs, too, and the man in the crowd laughs. So Apples stretches the joke.

"I'm so happy to see you're alive!"

"Me too, son!" the man in the crowd says, and the crowd howls.

Borden looks agitated by the whole business. Those

raincloud eyebrows lower and he shakes his head. If what's happening isn't a joke, then someone screwed up big time. The old man sits back down, and others pat him on the back. He's a natural. Dave gives the man an appreciate nod and then goes back to his jokes, the old stuff. That's when Mercy realizes what Dave's been doing all along: digging back into his earliest comedic bits to see if he can make a personal connection, possibly with his dad, who just might be alive in The Wellspring. And it worked. But the mist is too strong for them to recognize each other. They met, but then passed like strangers who shared small talk on a subway platform. They're happy but content-happy, not happy-happy, like they might be if truly reunited. Dave finishes his set, and of course drops the mic on the stage. Once a jerk always a jerk.

"I warmed them up for you, Rookie," Apples says to Mercy. "That dad thing was insane, right? Do you think they actually thought it was my dad?"

"Maybe Dave," Mercy says. "You did great out there."

"Time for you to clean up their adult diapers, Gorrison."

"It's so beautiful out there," Mercy says.

Borden nods, and a shot of nerves hits Mercy as she walks out onto the stage. She's never been in front of a crowd nearly this big. Cameras follow her from every direction, the crowd applauds and whistles; it's a thrill. But Mercy is keenly aware of the role she has to play. One slip that she's not on the mist and the masked guards stationed along the rows will likely jump up and tackle her right there in front of everyone. Borden needs happy and confident comics for the President's PR reel.

Mercy picks the microphone off the floor. "Big hand for Dave Apples. Didn't know I had to provide custodial services after your set, but I appreciate any work I can get." That earns an immediate laugh and Mercy can hear Apples cackle backstage too, appreciative of the mention. She places the microphone on the stand. It's not easy for Mercy to do jokes about anything but death. But realizing that they'll laugh at anything does ease her anxiety. "So, I've been dating… men, in case you wondered. And the new thing guys love to say on first dates is that they're 'empaths.' Some guy takes you to Del Taco on a crappy Tinder date and says, 'I'm an empath.' For those of you who don't follow modern jargon, an empath is someone with an almost supernatural ability to perceive and empathize with the emotions of others. This from a guy who let me know in the first five minutes that he calls his penis 'Girth Brooks.' Buddy, you're not an empath. Because if you were an empath you would know that I feel like you sound like an asshole when you call yourself an empath." Mercy tries not to act shocked by the massive wave of laughter. They're not laughing at her, but still, having a thousand people laugh at something you've just said feels incredible. During the laugh break Mercy notices one of the masked guards walking towards the center of the auditorium. He's bigger than the other guards and holds his gun Russian-style. Vlad walks to where the central machinery in located. It's a machine that Mercy thought was a lighting station but is actually a big pully like the one she'd seen dispense red mist in the halls. Her guess is that it's Vlad's job is to keep the crowd good and juiced so that they keep laughing.

"Maybe I'm just bad a dating," Mercy continues, trying not to get distracted. "Truth is I remained a virgin far too long. It almost happened in high school, but the guy chickened out, and then the next day he told everyone that I had an STD and that's why he didn't do it. But how do you get an STD without the D? So I stayed a virgin. And then I read that there are people selling their virginity online to the highest bidder. Some blonde eighteen-year got a cool million on eBay. So I went for it and put my virginity on eBay. Didn't work. In fact, the computer highly recommended I try a GoFundMe. When that didn't work, I did a garage sale. Everything must go!"

The place goes ballistic with laughter. It almost feels like Mercy is on the mist herself. But then she spots Vlad pulling a lever on the central machinery and when the mist falls from the ceiling, gently descending onto the crowd, Mercy can see clear as day that it's colored green and not red. Borden watches Mercy with an eagle eye side-stage so she tries to stay focused.

"I did eventually get the job done," Mercy say. "It was supposed to be a one-night stand but like an idiot I stayed. And when I woke up in the morning I did the one thing you're not supposed to do after sex—other than stay the night—I told him about my dream. Men are not deep, so he was bound to say something stupid and break my heart. I told him that in my dream Spike Lee was stalking me with a knife, but then he used the knife to fight off a monster that was about to attack me. Of course, there were a bunch of other crazy things that happened. I was in a swimming pool that wasn't a swimming pool, and my cousin Ray was making egg salad sandwich in a spacesuit, but the Spike Lee thing was the most memorable. Anyway, I tell him the dream about Spike Lee saving my life and he says, 'So in the end did he *Do The Right Thing*'?' And so after I had sex with Colby Foster for the second time, I asked him to be my Valentine."

It's a pretty lame joke, but thunderous applause come pouring out when Colby walks out on stage and gives a bashful bow to the crowd. The laughter is so loud it sounds more like howling. Mercy looks out to the crowd and sees faces veering from joy to pain—contorting, eyes rolling back, teeth grinding through laughter. Vlad's green mist has taken hold, and the crowd is being awoken painfully from their fantasy slumber into the shocked realization that they're in a prison auditorium and not the beautiful fantasy they'd inhabited seconds earlier. Vlad leaves the pulley and slips out the backdoor exit. Mercy looks side-stage and Borden is busy balling out some producer for letting Apples perform in front of his own father. But the camera crew, with their health masks blocking the green mist are not finding the shots of a smiling crowd that they need, and instead see miserable faces twisted in pain. Mercy pushes forward with her comedy, trying to bide her time before Borden becomes aware of what's going on.

"You know what's crazy?" Mercy asks. "White people complaining about white people on the internet. Kendrick Lamar did at a free concert in Compton, and my friend Jennifer Nussbaum and I were scrolling through the photos. I watched Jennifer put on a scrunchie, take a swig of a pumpkin spice latte, and say, 'Ugh, so many white people.'"

The crowd of Uninsured, now back in reality, watching an open mic comic tell a mediocre white-people joke, grimace their displeasure. They look around, finally realizing where they are, where they've been trapped, maybe for the first time in years. So, Mercy takes her chance before any new red mist can fall and bring them back to dreamland.

"You've all been tricked!" Mercy says into the microphone. "You've been taken away from your families because you're sick and Uninsured, and the government has been drugging you daily with a viral influencer mist to make you see a different reality. This is the true reality. This prison with armed guards and solitary cells. Not the beauty you've been seeing around you—that's the red mist. Your families mourn you every day. They pray to see you and beg for information about what's happening here, but the President won't tell. You're being lied to. They are liars. So revolt! Revolt! Fight back and free yourselves!"

Mercy sees Dave Apples running towards her onstage and she thinks he's going to tackle her, but instead Dave jumps off the stage and reaches the old man in the crowd who gave him a standing ovation, Stan. "Dad? Dad!" There's desperation in his voice, and the old man with sunken cheeks says, "David?" And they hug and cry, as the crowd around them turns to flee.

Guards rush in to maintain the chaos. Soldiers surround the pulley where Vlad was stationed, but when they attempt to repair it, more green mist falls, the truth serum and not the red mist.

"Eve Gorrison!" Mercy yells into the mic, scanning for those Minnie Mouse hair puffs. "Are you there? It's your daughter, Mercy!" Her voice is drowned out by blaring sirens, the barking of German Shepherds who run in from every exit door. Finally alerted, Borden rushes onstage with two guards and they tackle Mercy to the ground, and the microphone falls to the stage with a screech. Mercy kicks a guard in the face and then wiggles out of their arms. She grabs the microphone again and screams what she's dreamed of for so long. "Eve Gorrison! It's me! Your daughter, Mercy! I'm here to save you!"

The mic cuts off and Borden grabs Mercy's leg, but she pulls away and jumps off the stage, landing in Spider-man pose, full badass. An older woman in a headscarf runs over.

"I know Eve. She's in the Worker's Palace. She's always there." The woman points to the left of the auditorium. "Find the red door. And be careful—they'll kill you."

"Thank you," Mercy says, but the woman looks back horrified that Mercy would thank her for leading her to the Worker's Palace, whatever fresh hell that is.

The people of The Wellspring now awake from their hallucination, riot like their lives depend on it. When a guard levels a machine gun at them a chair is thrown that knocks him down, and the crowd rushes forward to maul him. The guard screams as his mask is ripped off and he is pummeled by the angry mob. When his German Sheppard bites one of the sick, an old lady takes the gun and shoots it dead.

Mercy runs out into the hallway. More green mist falls, and screams mix with sirens as the patients of The Wellspring awaken and pound on the doors of their solitary cells. A crowd of prisoners run with stolen keys and begin opening the cells, and the Sick run out into the fray, eager to fight the guards who've been keeping them drugged for years. But the SWAT guards double and triple in numbers, and bodies drop all over the place from gunfire.

"The Worker's Palace?" Mercy asks anyone who will listen. Mercy runs down another hallway and spots a red door with bars on the window.

Borden and an armed guard step out in front, and the guard levels his gun at her. "Give up, Mercy. It's over!"

Mercy keeps running and leaps into the air, flipping acrobatically towards them as bullets whiz past. But before Mercy can reach the soldier and maybe kill him with her bare hands, both the guard and Borden are tackled by a gang of enraged sick. They beat the guard as if he's a barrier separating them from freedom and grab his gun. Blood sprays on Borden, and Mercy drags out him of the scrum. He looks dazed, but momentarily thankful. Mercy takes Borden's hand, and there, still on his fingernail is the tiny mole that he scraped off Mercy's ear. Borden gives Mercy a crazy look as she picks the mole off his finger and places it gently back inside my ear. Then she swings and punches Borden so hard that teeth come flying out of his mouth and he collapses onto the floor.

"Dee?!" Mercy yells.

"She's alive!" Dee rejoices, and Mercy can hear Nan and Gus and Maude hoot in the background. "What the hell is going on over there?"

"Long story. I need entry into something called The Worker's Palace."

"Copy. I hacked into the grid. It's a labyrinth. But I got it," Dee says. Mercy hears her type fast. "Enter the red door and head down nine flights of stairs. I can get you in from there."

The red door buzzes open and Mercy rushes through it. She races down a metal stairwell as the sounds of gunfire and screams fade to the point where she can't hear a thing. Anyone down this far might be oblivious to the massive riot going on upstairs. Mercy arrives at the door nine floors down where there's a sign warning about steam burns.

"Open it," Mercy tell Dee.

The Worker's Palace, Mercy quickly discovers, is a massive underground warehouse where thousands of people in hospital gowns work diligently at metal picnic benches. Each bench has a steam pipe in the middle and there are buckets next to each worker. The workers dip their hands in the metal buckets to retrieve a kind of red Jell-O. They form the Jell-O into loose cubes and then place that cube into a metal ladle over the steam pipe in the middle of the table, which molds the cubes further. Once it has cooled into a perfect square, the workers place the completed red cube onto a conveyer belt that carries it away. It occurs to Mercy that this is some kind of production line and that they are producing the very mist that drugs them. At the far end of the factory are thousands of boxes ready for shipment.

But to where? If it's outside of The Wellspring it could mean a populace of zombies, and Mercy imagines that grim future, when amongst the workers she finds what she's looking for. A worker with perfect posture, high cheekbones and those two distinct hair puffs, just like Minnie Mouse. Mercy takes a first step towards our mother, already hatching a plan for escape.

"Amazing, isn't it?" a voice asks from behind. "How they work so diligently without a break. Cheaper that robots. I didn't think it was possibly myself, but just look. For once I'm proven wrong."

Mercy knows that voice—we all do. It's one of the most famous on earth, but also the one most of us hear in our nightmares. Mercy turns to strike Phyllis McCabe, The Plastic President, but something heavy hits her first—a sharp pain in the back of her head—and the world tilts sideways.

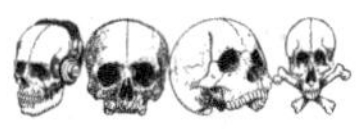

When Mercy comes to it's to that same perfect, smug smile that she's seen at White House press news briefings for years. Our fearless leader wears her famous white business suit. Her hair and makeup are flawless. Mercy is actually surprised that she looks so good under a prison cell's fluorescent lights.

"To what do I owe the honor, Madame President?" Mercy manages to ask.

"You're weak. Have some water." The President hands her a red cup.

"You going to roofie me too?" Mercy asks and waves

it off. "The crowbar to the head wasn't enough?"

McCabe grins. "Do you know why you're here, Mercy?"

"You didn't like my set?"

"Treason." The President seems to savor the word. "And multiple murders. Because of you many innocent people have died today."

"I have an alibi. I was on drugs." Mercy touches her ear, looking for Dee's mole.

The President smirks. "Looking for your friends? I've been told they'll be apprehended within the hour. That is unless they've already killed themselves, which is a distinct possibility. But whether they're dead or alive we'll find them and give them the burial they deserve."

"Grandma always wanted her ashes sprinkled into a double rainbow," Mercy says.

McCabe chuckles. "Such a kidder. Shame you're not clever enough to know what's good for you."

"What, walking around like a slave zombie? Is that what's good?"

"Zombies, no. These people are free, Mercy. Free from sickness. From misery. All of them were near terminal when they arrived here. They should be dead. But the brain is an amazing piece of machinery. A simple dosage of Viblotran Red and the human mind convinces the bodies into years of good health. We've discovered a way for the body to stave off disease through the mind manipulation. And it wasn't cheap."

"Then why not just give them the medicine at home? Why keep the sick here?"

"Clinical testing requires a controlled environment while we wait for the patent to be finalized. You'd be surprised how long that takes even for someone with my pull. But once we get it, the whole world will want our viral influencer. To heal but also, yes, to control.

The Chinese are chomping at the bit. Offered us billions and we haven't even shared the full effects."

"So this is about money?"

"It's about freedom from suffering."

"For the rich."

"We take away pain and prolong life for the Uninsured. The body is weak, Mercy—it feels stress and fear and breaks down under it. We make people healthy as long as the mind wants it. Then they can die happy."

"Is that what my mother wants? To die happy working as a slave in your factory?"

A strange look comes over McCabe's face as if she had not expected Mercy would be so direct. She turns to the guard and Mercy fully expects that he's going to beat her back to unconsciousness. Instead the guard leads a stooped woman into the cell. She's softer than Mercy remembered, but still beautiful. Those two pompoms stand proudly on her head but the rest of her seems defeated. Mom stares down at a Raggedy Anne doll that she holds in her hands. A little curly-haired doll with red cheeks and a dress.

"I'll leave you two alone," McCabe grins.

And then Mercy is alone with Mom. She really is alive.

"Mom," Mercy chokes out because she doesn't want to cry. She can see that Mom's eyes are dazed, deep on the mist. "It's me."

"This is my Mercy," Mom says in a voice that is sweet and almost childlike. She looks down at her doll, smiling bashfully. "She's with me all the time. She's only nine but she's precocious—cracks me up with her jokes. Mercy is such a funny little girl."

"Mom, I'm Mercy. Look at me." Her voice cracks again, tears welling.

"You're a woman," Mom says, and looks at Mercy,

confused. "A very beautiful woman. My Mercy is just a little girl."

"I've grown up. But I'm here. I've been looking for you for a really long time. And I've finally found you. Nan and Maude and Ester brought me up, and we always talked about you and kept you close in our hearts."

"They treat me really nicely here," Mom says. "I was deathly ill for a while, and they cured me. I didn't even have to pay a penny."

"I'm happy about that, Mom. I'm happy you're not sick anymore, but—"

"What do you do for work?" she asks. And Mercy gets the feeling that Mom's just trying to make small talk with a stranger.

"I'm a comic, Mom. I do stand-up comedy. Just like you and dad."

"You mean Golan?"

"Yes!" Mercy says, delighted that she remembers. "Golan, your husband, my dad. He was killed when they took you here. They shot him."

"A nice man. And a good dad to Mercy here." She continues to stroke her doll.

"I'm Mercy."

Mom's eyes grow suddenly skeptical. "You look like that killer."

"What?"

"The one who slices people's heads off so that they can never be healed at The Wellspring. You're that Ninja Girl. I saw a news report."

"No," Mercy is so taken aback that she almost chokes. "I'm a comic. I'm here because I won a contest. I make people laugh. I make people happy just like you and Dad made me."

"They showed a video on News Night. Said you would tell us you do comedy. But you're a killer." Mom looks back down at her doll. "This is my Mercy. She's nine years-old. And she's so funny. Tell her Mercy, but don't get too close. She's pretty but that's what a killer can look like too."

"Mom, wake up. They're drugging you; they've been drugging you every day." Tears stream down Mercy's face.

Mom holds the doll to her ear. "Mercy says you're sad. She says it would be okay if I lend her to you for a little while. Are you sure, Mercy?" she asks the doll again. Then she holds out the doll to Mercy.

"Wake up, mom!" Mercy screams. She's so frustrated that she just wants to shake her. Mom pulls back, genuinely frightened, and the doll drops between them. The movement is enough to alert the guards, and the door flies open, and two guards hold Mercy down on the cot. Mom looks frightened, like she just escaped a killer.

"Mercy's eyes are important," Mom stutters as she's led out. "Look in her eyes, okay? They always make me feel happy and free."

Mercy tries to lunge, but the guards push her back, hard. A gun is pointed at her head. When she settles, the guards exit the cell and lock the door.

Alone again, Mercy just fucking loses it, and I don't blame her. A deep guttural cry sounds from within, and the emotional pain is even worse than what she endured physically.

The cell door opens again, and President McCabe enters with her self-satisfied smile. "Ready to talk yet?" she asks. "We have so much we want to know."

Chapter 15

Mercy is given crayons and a stack of blank pages. She's told to confess everything and not to leave out a single detail. They threaten to take Mom off the red mist and then put her back on and off, over and over again, until the pain kills her. Does Mercy want to see that happen? The Plastic President would be happy to show her. Mercy knows that she would never come back from that. So, she writes. And writes. Until the crayons are nubs and they bring her another box. She changes some key info about the members of her Marvel Universe since as far as she knows they're still out there hiding for dear life, and she'd be damned if she's going to be the one to rat them out. But she admits to everything else. Her time working at Curated Ends. Fanny, Brandon, Carlos—the killing she did. She admits that sometimes she misses it, which surprises even her. Killing gave her no struggle. She was good at it. Not like comedy. Comedy is hard. Killing is easy.

Mercy stays locked in that cell for what seems like eternity. I can tell you from experience that time twists in solitary. An hour could be a month. Mercy was almost ready to ask for the red mist to escape reality. Worst of all, her tormentor, that stupid zombie doll

Mom left just glares at her from the floor. Her name is Mercy, and it occurs to Mercy maybe she's the real Mercy, and Mercy is a stuffed doll? The doll can't be manipulated by viral influencers, after all—she is what she is.

So Mercy says, 'screw it,' and talks to the doll. Asks it questions about our mother. According to Mercy, the doll answers. It knows how it all went down. It tells Mercy that they'd never captured anyone as mentally strong as our mother, and so they made her a special project. Mom allowed them to find out just how much red mist one person can take. Eventually, the doll gives enough information that Mercy decides to help her off the floor. She's been lying in an awkward position with her neck bent all that time. So Mercy picks up the doll and moves her to a more comfortable position on the cot. And eventually Mercy plays with her. Walks her around the cell in tiny circles, sleeps with her. And when Mercy is done writing her confession, she sits the doll down next to her and reads the entire thing from start to finish.

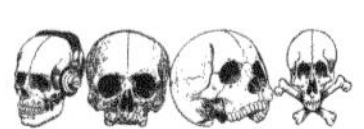

Mercy's cell door creaks open and she jumps out of sleep with a lurch. One of the things that makes people go mad in solitary is the uncertainty, and Mercy has built up in her mind a slew of terrible scenarios from torture to public execution to just being put to work on red mist. When two guards in full SWAT gear crowd her doorframe, Mercy makes herself as small as she can and buries her face in the doll.

"If you kill me I'll come back as a ghost and haunt you!" she says, because she heard it in a World War Two documentary, and it worked to save a prisoner's life from being executed by his Japanese captors. But the guards just stare at her for a while and then look at each other. Mercy has this horrible feeling that this is an illicit visit, and she's about to get a beating. "Expect disproportionate retaliation!"

One of the guards puts a finger over his visor to shush her. Of course, that's what he wants. Mercy is about to yell again when they move in on her. She's so scared and weak that she just folds. One guard picks her up and she's unable to fight back. The doll lays on the pillow, but it's become so meaningful that Mercy uses all her strength to reach out and grab it. If Mercy is about to be killed the doll needs to be with her for strength. The guards put Mercy in a burlap sack and the bigger guard just slings her over his shoulder and starts to walk. It's hot in the sack, but Mercy can breathe through the holes. She hears clicks and codes being typed and doors opening and closing. Through the fabric of the sack she sees halls filled with solitary cells and white walls. She sees other guards ahead stationed in front of a large door with a bolt lock.

"Official business," one of the guards says, but the voice is somehow familiar.

Mercy considers whether to scream out, when she hears a scuffle and she is lowered to the ground. Now Mercy hears shotgun blasts and men moan in pain until they are silenced by more gunshots. Mercy assumes she's next, so she bites against the fabric of the bag to escape when the top opens. Mercy sees two dead guards on the ground in front of her, blood oozing from their mouths. She grips her doll for security.

"Get up, idiot," the other guards says, and Mercy recognizes that Russian accent. Vlad pulls off his mask and Mercy worries that she's hallucinating again. Then the other guard pulls off his mask.

"Of all the fascist prison camps in all the American

wildernesses, and she had to choose this one," Nick says in classic Bogart.

"What are you doing here?" Mercy asks.

"Getting you the hell out of here," Nick replies. He picks her up and hugs her tight. "We've got help. The prisoners have been holding out in different parts of The Wellspring. Dee hacked into the computer system and has been blocking the red mist. But we don't have much time—they'll be able to go manual soon enough, and the doors are already on lockdown."

Vlad yanks at the huge metal door in front of them but even with his strength he only manages to move it a few inches. Nick pulls too and then Mercy uses what little strength she has as well.

Guards approach from down the hall. "Hey, you over there!"

"Now or never!" Nick says, and they tug hard, managing to open the door just wide enough to squeeze through. The door closes behind Mercy so fast it might have snapped off a limb. The guards give chase and pound on the door as Vlad reinforces the bolt locks.

Beyond the door is an enormous airport hangar. A row of black military vans are parked in the distance next to several helicopters outfitted with missiles. Vlad picks up Mercy and runs her to one of the vans, and Nick slides opens the side door. Vlad lays Mercy down in the back like a rag doll, clutching a rag doll. Mercy hates looking so weak in front of Nick but she's barely able to sit up.

"Eat." Vlad throws Mercy a bag of McDonald's.

"Filet O' Fish, really?" Mercy complains, and Vlad gives her a look.

Nick pulls out a laptop. He cups his hand to his ear, and Mercy can tell that he's taking orders from Dee. "Stop yelling at me," Nick says. "It's not working. I've pressed it twice and the hangar won't open." But then a loud screech sounds, and the main hangar door begins to rise slowly. "Oh, wait. It's working now."

Morning light spills into the hangar as the door inches up. It's the first natural light Mercy has seen since she's been inside, and it's blinding. Vlad moves the van forward slowly, waiting for the hangar door to rise high enough for the van to fit. It's halfway when the bolt-locked door that they struggled with bursts open, and a stream of armed guards run into the hangar.

"Gun it!" Nick says.

Vlad puts pedal to metal as the line of guards raise their machine guns and open fire, and the van is hit by a wave of bullets. The bulletproof glass holds, but bullets imbed in the glass and cracks form. Vlad screeches to a halt behind a tank. "New strategy," Vlad says.

"Playing dead?"

The guards walk in lockstep towards the exit door and form a barrier. Other soldiers jump in military vehicles and start a blockade. Mercy squeezes her doll.

"We had a good run," she says.

"Not so fast," Nick says, and points to the far end of the hangar.

A stream of sick patients rush in. They wear hospital gowns, but some have SWAT helmets and carry shields and machine guns. They turn to the line of soldiers and open fire.

"Go! Go!" Nick says and Vlad guns it again.

The hangar door is almost high enough to squeeze through, but a SWAT guard rushes to the manual lever and pulls it, which triggers the door to reverse, and daylight fades. Vlad swerves around, barely avoiding the Sick, but also knocking down a few guards. Mercy tumbles in the backseat. The rioting prisoners fight with sticks and bare hands. They run up to the guard controlling the hangar door and tackle him. Vlad swerves again as the door rises. Mercy looks out the cracked window and sees that it's our Mom holding the lever. Those two Minnie Mouse hair puffs, and a posture that is far from stooped and childlike but now strong and confident. Total badass. An armed guard reloads his gun and point it at her.

"Mom, look out!" Mercy shouts.

The van races forward, sending the guard over the windshield. As they reach the exit Mercy catches our mother's eyes. Mom smiles broadly, winking proudly at her daughter, but then her smile fades. She looks down at her stomach where a patch of red has formed on her hospital gown. She appears more annoyed than hurt, like now she has to have it dry cleaned, but then she's hit again. Mercy watches Mom stumble, keeping her hand steady on the lever despite the pain. Finally, Mom lets go as the van makes it out into the sunshine, into open air. She slides down the wall, limp.

"Mom!" Mercy shouts.

"Hold tight!" Nick yells.

The van roars onto a slick road under heavy gunfire. The wheels screech to gain footing. It's so bright outside Mercy can barely see, but it's clear that the patient riot has spilled out of The Wellspring building. There's fire and smoke from a crashed military helicopter and carnage everywhere. Patients in hospital gowns run ragged in all directions and Mercy wonders if satellites can pick up the images for distribution.

"How do we get out of here?" Vlad asks.

"Dee's working on it," Nick says, and his fingers fly on the keyboard. "There are no maps here. Where the hell are we anyway?"

"We have to wing it then," Vlad says. "You be my eyes."

And that's when it dawns on Mercy. She holds Mercy the doll out to Nick. "Scan the doll's eyes."

"Mercy, you're freaking out."

"Scan them!" she yells.

Nick gives her a crazy look but when he holds the doll's face up to the computer scanner there are a series of beeps. "Dee, are you seeing this?" Mercy peeks at his screen, and a whole slew of maps pop up. "Well, then decode them. Fast!"

Vlad races aimlessly along the road. Military vehicles give chase, taking aim with their gunners. A black military helicopter swoops down in front of them.

"I need news!" Vlad yells.

"There's a forest entry," Nick shouts, hand to his earpiece. "To the right. A maintenance truck next to a yellow flag. Get to the truck and drive into the trees directly next to it."

Vlad screeches to the right. Ahead of them is a wall of trees and a truck parked off in the distance. The guards must know what they're up to because gunfire increases, bullets pinging against the back of the van, finally shattering the windows. Glass sprays onto Mercy, who is thrown around as Vlad swerves to regain control. The helicopter hovers low in front of them like a massive vulture. It tilts its missile-snout and fires, but the missile skids along the slick pavement and bounces just high enough to miss the van.

"The entrance!" Nick points. "Dee says there's a digital force field. It will close if we can breach it first."

"How do you close a forest?"

"Something tells me we're about to find out."

The helicopter swoops around, making another attack from behind, and a new fleet of military vehicles give chase, machine guns blasting.

"Hold on!" Nick screams.

The van reaches the truck and takes flight into the forest just as the helicopter fires another missile. A green light explodes around the van, and Mercy sees a digital force-field shut behind them and the military vehicles that follow explode in flames. The feeling of evading the soldiers provides only momentary relief before the van meets the lip of the forest edge and gravity takes hold. The van crashes roughly onto the forest floor and Vlad slams on the breaks, but momentum carries them. They barrel forward past elephant-sized tree trunks that would tear the van apart if they hit, and down towards the even more terrifying sight of an oncoming cliff with jagged rocks jutting up below.

"Mother Russia, save me!" Vlad screams.

The van hits a boulder and flips. It careens towards the cliff's edge. Mercy holds on for dear life as they tumble through a cloud of rocks and smoke, and finally crash inches from the edge. The van teeters towards death.

Mercy hears Vlad whimper as he finally opens his eyes. He takes a long, slow breath, and ever-so-carefully puts the van in reverse, inching it back to solid ground. "Thank you, Mother Russia," Vlad says, a single tear lining his face.

They sit there in silence. A long wooden bridge stretches out in front of them, connecting one side of the forest to the other. Underneath is a deadly chasm of scabrous rocks. But it's their only way forward, so Vlad rolls the van slowly onto it. The van's punctured wheels creak the wooden planks as they make the journey across the bridge. On the other side a second forest engulfs them, this one darker and cooler under a thick canopy of trees. Helicopters rumble above but are out of sight under the foliage.

"Where the hell are we now?" Nick asks.

"We're stuck," Vlad says as the van's motor sputters to a stop.

Mercy looks out into the forest and it's somehow familiar to her. The trees are like the ones she'd imagined in her drug-infused haze. Colorful birds twitter on treetops. Mercy rubs her eyes, praying this isn't the mist playing tricks on her, and that's when she sees a rustle in the foliage. Something that's invisible but also that moves. Camouflaged soldiers with machine guns jump out into the clearing and surround the van from every direction.

"Gun it!" Nick says.

But the engine just clicks weakly, dead. The soldiers move in, and the only reason Mercy can think of why they aren't opening fire is that they want them alive. She thinks to kill Vlad and Nick right then and there because she doesn't want them tortured like she was. Instead she says, "When the door opens, we fight." She gives Nick a sorrowful look. She led him to this—to an early death in a strange forest. A machine gun taps at the van door, beckoning them to come out peacefully or die. Vlad slowly opens his door and he's sucked out of his seat as if by a giant vacuum. Then Nick's door opens, and he's pulled out too. Finally, the side door slides open and soldiers peer in, guns leveled at Mercy's head.

"I'm not telling you shit!" Mercy yells. "You'll just have to kill me."

Mercy is yanked out of her seat and thrown onto the muddy ground next to Vlad and Nick. Guns point at their heads. The biggest one looks down at Mercy like he's considering her end. He leans over and grabs the doll from her hands.

"You steal this from inside?" the masked man asks in a voice that is low and gruff.

"Yeah," Mercy replies. "But I already scanned her eyes, so you've already lost, motherfucker!"

The soldier considers the doll carefully, then flips it over and massages its backside. Nick and Vlad give each other a strange look.

"Who are you?" the soldier asks Mercy, and she's

nudged with gun barrels.

"Mercy Gorrison, stand-up comedian – these are my joke writers."

"Why are you driving a Dog Van?" he says and raises his gun to her face.

Nick is about to admit his position, like an idiot.

"Stole it," Mercy cuts in.

"Where'd you get the doll?"

"My mother gave it to me," Mercy admits because she's dead anyway. "Eve Gorrison. A great hero of the Resistance."

There's an audible gasp from the group of soldiers. "Bullshit," the leader says, and now he's pointing his gun at Mercy's face. "One more lie and you're dead…"

"Ask me anything," Mercy says.

"Eve Gorrison ran a comedy club," the soldier says. "What was it called?"

"Misses Nice's Comedy Bra," Mercy replies.

Again, the soldiers gasp. There's another long pause as they mumble to each other. Nick shoots Mercy a confused look.

"I'm Miggs," The soldier says and pulls off his mask. "An old friend of your mother and father." He's old but bearded and handsome with deep set eyes and a long scar along his brow. "We all are." He motions to the other soldiers, who lower their guns, and give an awkward half-wave as they remove their masks. "She used to give us stage time at the club. We've been trying to get her out of The Wellspring for years."

"Wait, you're… comics?"

"We don't seem funny to you?" Miggs asks. "We do an open mic thing by the bridge on Tuesday nights. Pretty amateur, mainly…"

"Not amateur anymore," Mercy hears a familiar voice cut in from amongst the soldiers. "They've finally got a mainstager." The soldier peels off his mask. It's

Dave Apples. Standing next to him, Colby. Mercy tries to speak but all that comes out is a stuttering version of, "B-u-t how?"

"We snuck out during the riot. My dad said he heard about the forest, and we made a run for it." Mercy sees that next to Apples is the stooped, old man from the crowd, Stan. And then next to Colby, snuggling up to him is the dancer who Mercy thought was a spy. Colby leans over and kisses her cheek.

"I kinda like it here," says Colby. "Puns kills in the jungle."

Mercy rushes forward and hugs Colby. And then she hugs Dave Apples too. Vlad and Nick slowly get up off the ground and brush the muck off their clothes.

"We've got to get you out of here," Miggs says. "You're bringing too much heat."

And indeed, the rumble of helicopters above gets more insistent, and the green shield flashes consistently as military vans try to crash through, only to explode in flames. Miggs gives the soldiers a sign and they pick up their guns and rush off towards the wreckage. Miggs, Colby, Dave Apples, and several other soldiers lead Mercy, Vlad and Nick down a path deeper into the forest. They slide down mossy rocks and across a rushing river until they arrive at an enormous, ancient oak tree.

"We're here," Miggs says.

And before Mercy can ask, "Where?" he holds up Mercy the Doll and rips open her ear. From inside, Miggs pulls out a microchip in a plastic case. He places the chip on the side of his phone and the screen lights up.

"Son of a bitch, she did it," Miggs says, shaking his head. He tosses the doll back to Mercy, now with a ripped ear. "What I have will keep those helicopters at bay for a while. Whatever else is in this doll isn't for us.

Guard it with your life, Mercy. What's in that doll is more valuable than you can imagine."

A hidden door opens in the oak tree and Miggs motions them in. Mercy takes the doll, hugs Colby and Dave Apples again, and then enters the dark space within, along with Vlad and Nick. A long, curved staircase takes them down into cool darkness, and they descend until they reach a nearly pitch-black room at the bottom. There, a rusty rail car sits at the edge of a dark tunnel.

"This probably isn't going to be fun," Nick says.

The three of them climb into the rail car, with Vlad on one side, and Mercy sort of draped over Nick. Vlad reaches for the lever on top, and the rail car jolts forward into the tunnel. Nick closes the metal lid over them, which thank God has bullet holes, so they can breathe pretty well. Still, it's like being inside a crowded tomb. The railcar stumbles forward, and they ride that way for hours, like on the crappiest rollercoaster ever. The twists are so sudden that Mercy feels sick, but she does her best not to vomit on Nick or Vlad, who are clearly trying to breathe through this experience the best they can. It takes so long that Mercy goes to sleep or faints, who can tell anymore. She wakes up to Nick nudging her.

"Be ready for anything," he says.

The rail car screeches to a stop. Vlad pushes open the lid and the three of them climb out. They're in some kind of creepy warehouse with graffiti on the walls and windows covered in duct tape and cardboard. Rats gnaw on garbage in the corner.

"I hate rollercoasters," Vlad grunts, and sprays puke all over the dirty ground.

Nick and Mercy can't help but grin at this huge immovable man whose kryptonite turns out to be rail car rides.

"Psst!" a voice calls out from above. It's a little girl in the rafters. She's filthy and tiny, crouched, and looking down at them. "You have Mercy?"

Mercy holds up the doll.

"Follow me," the girl says.

They ask no questions, just follow the little girl to the back of the warehouse. She motions them towards a window that is blacked out. She peels off a small piece of duct tape, giving them a view of outside. The streets are still and mostly quiet. Pre-dawn light glimmers off the old office buildings.

"They're waiting for you at the subway station across the street," the little girl says. "You'll be safe there. Wait behind that green dumpster until you get a sign." She then takes out a shoebox and pulls out two handguns. Vlad reels back, but then she hands him one and gives the other to Nick.

"What about me?" Mercy asks.

"You protect the doll," the girl says. "A gun will only distract you."

The girl opens the window and Vlad, Nick and Mercy climb out onto the street where across the way is the dumpster where they've been instructed to go. They crouch low and walk shoulder-to-shoulder. The streets are mostly empty, but a man sets up a coffee stand on the corner. He raises his finger to his lips to let them know he's staying quiet, and so should they.

"Did she say what sign we're waiting for?" Nick asks.

"Quiet," Vlad says.

A low rumble sounds from above, and two black military helicopters emerge from behind an office building and hover above the streets. They turn in tandem towards Vlad, Nick and Mercy's spot at the dumpster.

"Maybe they don't see us?" Nick whispers, but

Vlad points his finger to the coffee guy, who is quietly pulling his cart out of harm's way.

"Wonder how much they paid him?" Vlad asks.

Military vans screech in from every direction and blockade the streets around the dumpster. In an instant they're surrounded from sky and land, and all they have is two rusty handguns to ward them off.

"Put down your guns and surrender!" A megaphone blasts from one of the trucks. "Place the doll on the ground, put your hands on your head. If you do not comply in ten seconds, we will be forced to open fire."

"They won't shoot," Mercy says. "They need what's in that doll too badly."

Mercy looks down at the doll, maybe hoping for guidance, when she notices a sliver of light flickering off the doll's face. Then a red beam settles on its forehead. Mercy looks up and sees that the light is coming from a high window by the alley.

"Get under the dumpster," Mercy says to Nick and Vlad. "They're going to fight back."

"How do you know?"

"Just go!"

They scramble underneath the dumpster and take cover, and at once a blast of red-hot light flashes from the alley and a sonic boom lifts them off the pavement as a missile fires. The helicopters swerve to avoid the shot and the missile instead hits the row of military vehicles, which explode in the air. The helicopters try to get steady, but their tails catch and they both crash down into the streets. Flaming metal explodes in the air and a helicopter blade flies underneath the dumpster almost slicing Nick's head clear off his body. Mercy squirms away from a clump of molten debris. Gunfire breaks out as men and women with machine guns and filthy clothes emerge from every alley. Mercy spots the little girl with the braids in an alley near the subway.

She waves them over.

"We have to run," Mercy says. "Now!"

Mercy grabs Nick's hand and they race forward through heavy gunfire. A Jeep mounted with a machine gun screeches to a stop in front of them, blocking their path to the alley. An enormous gunman in an army helmet climbs onto the roof and points his gunner, daring them to move an inch further. They stop, hands in the air, and the gunner leans in to take better aim. Vlad leaps in front of Mercy and falls to the ground with a thud—blood soaks his chest.

"Vlad, no!"

The gunner reloads when two resistance fighters jump onboard and stab him in the back. The gunner collapses onto his gun, which sprays bullets in every direction. The rebels hurl his body off the vehicle and take control of the gun, now pointing it at the enemy.

"We have cover!" Mercy yells.

"Leave me." Vlad waves her off.

"Not in a million years."

Nick and Mercy pull Vlad off the ground, and he winces in pain. It takes everything they have to lift him. They stumble forward through a rain of bullets and fall into the alley. There, a big metal door swings open and when Mercy sees who's there to the greet them, by instinct she says, "Whiskey. And by whiskey, I mean absinthe. And by absinthe, I mean cocaine. And by cocaine, I mean…"

"Shut up you idiot!" Gus says, and then helps to lift Vlad.

Inside is an abandoned subway station where tiled walls are riddled with bullet holes and lights flicker on and off. Resistant fighters rush around, readying weapons for battle. There's been rumors that The Resistance owns the subways and that's why the government keeps reporting rat infestations down there.

A woman approaches, carrying a medical kit, and tends to Vlad. "He's lost a lot of blood," she says, inspecting his wounds. "Leave us. Frank is waiting for you downstairs."

"Who's Frank?" Nick asks.

"Promise me you'll save him," Mercy pleads with the doctor.

"No promises," she replies. "But I'll try."

Mercy kisses Vlad's damp forehead and he gives her a look that says get the hell out of here.

Mercy, Nick and Gus rush off through a broken turnstile and past the cracked glass of the pay station onto a long escalator. At the bottom is an abandoned subway platform. Gus leads Nick and Mercy onto the rails and through a dimly lit tunnel until they arrive at the back of an old subway car. Inside, it's like a war room. Maps are taped over windows. Computers beep and whirr. Machine guns and ammo are stacked next to shelves of crusty 'health trackers' that have been removed from human flesh. They walk from car to car, passing wounded fighters who look like they've been fighting for years. They nod at Mercy and Nick as they walk by, like somehow, they've been with them all along.

In the final subway car there's a makeshift office, and a tall woman with silver hair and dark eyes sits behind a wooden desk next to an antique globe. "Welcome, Mercy Gorrison." The woman smiles. "And Nick."

"You're Frank?" Mercy asks.

"I am," she says. "And while I'd love to make small talk, you've got something that I need." She looks down at the doll in Mercy's hand.

And that's when I decide to make my grand entrance. It takes Mercy completely by surprise. "Still playing with dolls, huh, Little Sis?" It's the only thing I can think of to stop myself from crying.

Chapter 16

Mercy the Doll, as it turns out, was just the weapon The Resistance needed to take down President McCabe once and for all. I worked with Dee to decode what was left of the files, and it laid out the inner workings of The Wellspring, top to bottom. Mom had attached digital maps as well as codes that could empower anyone with Wi-Fi to shut the place down. But there was videos evidence too— hours of footage of patients being admitted, beaten and experimented on. And of them fighting back until the red mist drugged them into compliance. Mom had been stowing away information since the very beginning and storing it all inside her little doll, so it was pretty damning stuff. The only thing no one could figure out was how Mom was able to keep her mind so strong even with reality melded into fantasy for so many years of red mist.

Ironically, the President's real downfall wasn't the depraved prison camp she'd been running for years. They got her on a finance technicality. For plans to manufacture, sell, and profit massively from the sale of Viblotran Red to the Chinese. Under the Foreign Emoluments Clause, a President can't profit from the power of the Presidency, and Congress finally had the courage to impeach. McCabe pulled every trick in her book to evade them, but once her inner circle sensed they'd be thrown to the wolves, internal documents leaked and then the shit really hit the fan. The President took one final swing to appeal to her base— a live broadcast from the Oval Office where she denied everything and blamed it all on the Chinese and their quest to destroy America with propaganda. The lighting was perfect, and Phyllis McCabe was impressively composed. And it just might have worked had a subversive Production Assistant on the TV crew not hacked into the broadcast and superimposed that legendary prison cell footage in the corner of the screen. It was the footage that would make Mercy famous, or infamous at least. Seen through the doll's eyes, and held by our mother who stood just outside Mercy's cell door, it was a recording of the President laying out her entire evil plan, down to details about who she was going to sell the red mist to and why. TV viewers got to see not only that video but McCabe reacting live to seeing it super-imposed on her TV monitor. She had the meltdown of a lifetime and threw a chair at the cameraman that broke his nose. The broadcast cut off there but not after millions of viewers had captured the footage and spread it online.

The dissolution of the government still took a while. The military tried to negotiate a peace treaty with The Resistance who told them where they could shove it. But eventually hospitals opened back up and the sick were treated by real doctors, and later, even wounded resistance fighters were allowed in.

So, did America start a revolution in Health Care that opened to the poor? It did not. But it did start "Congressional Oversight Committees," and closed down The Wellspring for good.

Dee and her mother were instrumental in tracking

down McCabe's hidden accounts, and as a reward, Dee was hired into the Federal Forensic Accounting Division. There, Dee was like a kid in a candy store. She even hired Gus as her personal security detail.

Vlad eventually recovered from his gunshot wounds and is back teaching self-defense, toughening up the next generation of fighters with knuckle push-ups.

As for my sister Mercy, well, part of what was recorded in the doll's eyes was her reading her entire confession out loud, the one I transcribed. In it, Mercy details her killings at Curated Ends, making an easy case for the prosecutor. They had to arrest her for that based on precedent, and few could blame them (not even Nan and Maude), though they did have leniency in sentencing, so she got minimum-security prison. Nick and Mercy got a quickie marriage before sentencing so that Nick could make conjugal visits when he isn't working his new job at a hospice for sick pets.

Life isn't so bad for my little sister, Mercy. Sometimes the Warden lets her do comedy and I got a contract job working the audio system just so I could hear her live. At first it was just an open mic thing in her cell block. But she kept telling him she's ready for the mainstage, so today he's finally letting that happen.

So Mercy is standing at the side of the stage (no velvet curtains in prison!), taking one last look over her joke sheet before she heads on. She's built about twenty solid minutes of material and it's not all about death, either. Maybe prison has given her time to lighten the hell up a little? One reason is the feeling she has right now as she gives me two thumbs up, takes center stage, and says those four words that every comedian must, regardless of where they are or what strange twists life serves them.

"How's everybody doing tonight?"

I would like to thank the incredible team at Madness House Press. To Publishing Editor John Baltisberger – a creative inspiration, champion of indie writers, and all-around mensch. To Maxwell Bauman, the editor of this book, who cares deeply about writing, and always makes everything better. Thank you for your hard work, dedication, and care.

To Luke Spooner for creating the stunning cover art. Doesn't get much better than having an artist whose work you so admire bring your writing alive in a painting. Thank you.

Thanks to Ethan T. Berlin's Comedy Writing Workshop, where I wrote most of the jokes in this book, and where I always received encouragement and helpful tags.

To Liv Breads in Millburn, NJ, the coffee shop where I wrote this book on early mornings. Thanks for the strong coffee, and for giving me a place to write when I needed it most.

And to my special ones: Liz Blazer and Evan Oliver. Love you both.

--Jeff Oliver
March 2024

Who is Jeff Oliver?

Jeff Oliver is the author of four novels, including The Two-Plate Solution, Scapegoated, and the forthcoming Madness Heart Press Pocket Book, Yentl Goes Mental. A veteran TV producer and developer, he lives in Maplewood, NJ with his family.

More Books from

Madness Heart Press

A Harrowing of Flesh & Spirit by Zach Rosenberg
isbn: 978-1-955745-66-6

Hauntologies/PLAYS by Ben Arzate
isbn: 978-1-955745-23-9

Mania by Lucas Mangum
isbn: 978-1-087893-98-3

City of Spores by Austin Shirey
isbn: 978-1-955745-63-5

Scapegoated by Jeff Oliver
isbn: 978-1-955745-14-7

Whispers of the Dead Saint by John Baltisberger
isbn: 978-1-955745-39-0

Giant Robots of Babel by Maxwell Bauman
isbn: 978-1-955745-07-9

GUSH by Gina Ranalli
isbn: 978-1-955745-47-5

Porcelain by Nate Southard
isbn: 978-1-955745-89-5